"Let's make a deal," Amy whispered in Jared's ear. *"I will allow you to help with the wedding, but only on one condition. You do the work yourself. Not your PA, not your events planner, not your brilliant admin team. You. Or is the great Jared Shaw scared of getting his hands dirty?"*

And she looked up at him with the sweetest, most adoring openmouthed smile, complete with fluttering eyelashes for the benefit of the onlookers.

"Do we have a deal? Squeeze once for yes and twice for no."

Jared tightened his grip on Amy's waist.

There was no backing out.

He squeezed. Once.

Dear Reader,

Thank you for choosing *Always the Bridesmaid*.

One of my fondest childhood memories is visiting the public library with my mother, and staring in awe at the shelves packed with wonderful bright covers. Books opened up a world of excitement, danger and romance for me, and I have been a compulsive reader ever since.

That sense of wonder has never left me.

Since then I have read some of my favorite Harlequin novels so many times that the pages are held together with staples!

I am especially thrilled that my first Harlequin novel will be published in 2009.

Many congratulations to Harlequin on the first sixty years. Long may we continue to delight readers.

I would love to hear from my readers, and you can get in touch and find out my latest news by visiting www.ninaharrington.com.

Nina Harrington

NINA HARRINGTON

Always the Bridesmaid

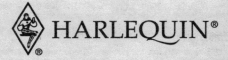

HARLEQUIN®

TORONTO • NEW YORK • LONDON
AMSTERDAM • PARIS • SYDNEY • HAMBURG
STOCKHOLM • ATHENS • TOKYO • MILAN • MADRID
PRAGUE • WARSAW • BUDAPEST • AUCKLAND

Recycling programs
for this product may
not exist in your area.

ISBN-13: 978-0-373-17600-7

ALWAYS THE BRIDESMAID

First North American Publication 2009.

Copyright © 2009 by Nina Harrington.

www.eHarlequin.com

Printed in U.S.A.

Nina Harrington grew up in rural Northumberland, England, and decided at the age of eleven that she was going to be a librarian— because then she could read all of the books in the public library whenever she wanted! Since then she has been a shop assistant, a community pharmacist, a technical writer, a university lecturer, a volcano walker and an industrial scientist, before taking a career break to realize her dream of being a fiction writer. When she is not creating stories that make her readers smile, her hobbies are cooking, eating, enjoying good wine—and talking, for which she has had specialist training.

This is Nina's debut book!

To all the wonderful writers
in the Romantic Novelists' Association,
who made this book possible.

CHAPTER ONE

AMY EDLER had three problems. All female. And all of them were demanding her attention at that very minute—or there would be tears. Added to that, she had a telephone crammed between her shoulderblade and her ear, a bakery full of customers, and the air-conditioning had chosen the hottest day in June to start playing the maracas.

It had been Trixi's idea to offer two of Amy's problems a chance to ice the chocolate cupcakes—a treat for the other girls at the children's home.

Only this was *real* chocolate icing. And these two problems were eleven-years old.

Big mistake.

Huge.

Amy tried to catch Trixi's eye, but her catering student was too busy chatting to the last of the customers for the day to help her judge the best-iced cupcake contest.

She looked down at the trembling lip of the taller girl, glanced swiftly at the still liquid icing, which had flooded the paper cases and pooled out over the plate, and decided that her phone call could wait.

'I think these cakes were too warm from the oven. But look at that shine! They look delicious.'

The little girl gave her a warm, closed-mouthed grin and shrugged her shoulders in delight. But then her friend started sniffing. She had decided to freeze the icing to help it set, and now two thick slabs of brown fudge lay on top of each cake.

Amy quickly scooped up the plate, popped it into the microwave for twenty seconds, then spread the now soft luscious frosting into smooth layers.

Their owner's mouth formed a perfect 'Wow', and then broke into a toothy grin.

Amy bent down to whisper. 'I won't tell if you don't. They're perfect! And well done for thinking ahead.' She stood up, head high. 'I don't think I can judge this icing competition properly today, because of the heat—but how about next time? Was that a yes? Brilliant. Now, I would be in serious trouble if I let you go home like that, so it's time to wash your fingers. Go on—I'll guard your cakes!'

She couldn't help but grin as the delighted little girls joined their pals in a gaggle of excited chatter, filling the room instantly with laughter.

This was just how she had imagined it would be.

Her bakery and her kitchen filled with happy children.

A sigh escaped from somewhere deep inside before she swallowed it down.

One day soon.

She knew she could offer a child a loving home. But first she had to pass the assessment process and prove that she could be a responsible single parent before she could even hope to adopt.

Amy dropped her shoulders and gave herself a mental shake. No time to dwell on that dream. Not at six o'clock on a Friday afternoon, when she still had to deal with problem female number three.

Which, in theory, should not have been a problem at all, since her friend Lucy Shaw had gone out of her way to find the most experienced wedding planner in London to organise her big day.

Pity that this planner was not answering any of her telephones.

Amy counted out the beeps on the answering machine. 'Hello, Clarissa, it's Amy Edler here, at Edlers Bakery. Sorry to hassle you, but you did say that you would get back to me about the orchids for the Shaw-Gerard wedding. Please call me as soon as you can.' Then she added a cheery, 'Thank you!'

Amy exhaled a slow calming breath, before squeezing her eyes tight shut and pressing the cool telephone to her forehead.

I have the situation under control. The wedding is not until next Saturday.

The cake is going to be perfect. The wedding is going to be perfect.

I can make sugar orchids in any colour Lucy likes. Not a problem.

And I will be transformed from a humble baker into a lovely bridesmaid.

This was going to have to be her mantra for the next seven days.

Of course it was entirely her own fault for offering to make Lucy's wedding cake in the first place. The perfect cake, as her personal wedding present for two of the best friends she had in this world.

It had to be chocolate, of course. *No dried fruit, thank you. Shudder.*

And decorated with sugar flowers the same colour as Lucy's bouquet—*no sludgy icing to drip on the designer wedding dress.*

And three tiers, made from different types of chocolate—*all organic, of course.*

Thank you for the sleepless nights, Lucy.

A peal of bright girly laughter broke through her thoughts, and Amy opened her eyes as the last girls from her after-school club waved on their way out, their arms laden with cupcakes and muffins, and their care worker tried her hardest to persuade them to get back to the home for dinner. It was like herding cattle.

'Make sure some of those make it back!' Amy called after them.

'Not a chance. Sorry we can't stay to clear up,' the flustered care worker answered.

Amy grinned as the gigglers swept out of the kitchen and into the shop, taking with them the life and energy she loved, and leaving behind… Oh, dear.

With one shake of the head she was on her feet. Time to get busy.

Jared Shaw weaved his way along a pavement crammed with commuters rushing to get home on a hot Friday evening, before taking advantage of a red traffic light to jog across the road between the cars, messenger bikes and cabs to a row of three small shops.

Not that much had changed over the past eighteen years.

The newsagent where he had bought his first car magazines was still there, but the ironmonger who had mended their leaking tap in exchange for one of his father's silk ties had been replaced by a swish-looking estate agency.

He couldn't help but smile at the irony of that.

Friends in the trade had laughed out loud when Haywood and Shaw had bought properties in this part of London. *'No profit there, mate.'*

Well, he had proved them wrong. Many times over.

But it was the last shop in the row he was interested in. Edlers Bakery shone out from the brick and stone surroundings, with its familiar navy and white awning.

How many times had he pressed his nose against the cold glass, jaw slack, gazing at the cream and chocolate treats which might as well have been objects on a distant planet to a boy without the money in his pocket to buy them?

A giggling little girl on a tricycle trundled towards him on the pavement, followed by a man of about his age. She looked so like the young Lucy he caught his breath. Long straight blonde hair, blue eyes, and a smile that could melt the hardest heart.

Jared pushed back his shoulders, sensing the tension.

Perhaps this was a mistake? Too many ghosts lived on these streets.

There was only one person who could have persuaded him to come back to this part of the city.

'It will only take five minutes to pop in and say hello to my pal Amy Edler,' his sister Lucy had said, in her special pleading voice. 'Just to make sure that she's not running herself ragged trying to organise my wedding. She has enough to do making my cake, and you are going to be in London anyway!'

Right. *Thank you, sis*. He had just worked a ninety-hour week. The last thing he wanted to do was chat to a frilly bridesmaid about wedding cakes when he was already paying for the most expensive wedding planner in the city.

He earned the money, and Lucy and their mother spent it for him.

But when could he ever refuse his baby sister anything?

She was the only girl who knew exactly how to twist him around her little finger! He had somehow agreed to make a detour on his way back to his penthouse apartment from Heathrow airport and make time to chat to her friend Amy, when all he truly wanted was a good Internet connection to catch up with the New York office before they closed for the weekend.

Time to find out if Lucy had been right to trust Amy Edler...

A bell tinkled over his head as Jared swung open the door onto the terracotta-tiled floor of Edlers Bakery—just in time to hold it open for an elderly couple who were still laughing as they thanked him, their hands curled around the handles of Edlers Bakery bags, before chortling their way down the street.

As he turned back to face the counter, his senses were hit with a solid wall of lively chatter, bright lights and the aroma of baked goods. Spices and vanilla, combined with the unique tang of burnt sugar and buttery pastry and fresh-baked bread.

The overall effect was overpowering, compared to the metallic bitter diesel fumes from the black cabs and London buses on the other side of the glass, and as he inhaled a couple of times to steady his senses he picked up some type of perfume—not from the flowers he was carrying. Roses? Oranges?

He glanced around the room, his property developer's brain taking in the cream and navy paintwork broken up by pale wood shelving.

It was a world away from the dingy brown wallpaper and cracked wooden shelves of the old Edlers Bakery he remembered. Yellowing torn posters for flour and fizzy drinks had been replaced with clean smooth walls in warm colours.

The overall effect was modern, stylish, but welcoming. Interesting. He should mention the idea to his design team.

Someone here clearly had an eye for texture and colour.

The bread was laid out behind the counter, but it was the display of cakes and pastries that had been designed to tantalize. Under pristine curved glass was a collection of amazing individual cakes, tarts and scones which any French patisserie would have been proud of. Most of the trays were almost empty.

Right on cue, the navy curtain swished open, and Jared looked into the brown eyes of a teenage girl in a smart navy apron over a T-shirt decorated with a strange combination of brown and white splodges. A small white badge declared that he was looking at 'Trixi'.

'Hello, handsome. Those for me?'

Jared was so taken aback that she had to gesture towards the bouquet of exotic blooms in his left hand before he realised what she was referring to. He had heard of casual customer service, but this took it to the next level.

'Sorry. No. I'm looking for Miss Amy Edler. Is she available today?'

Without any further warning, Trixi turned away from Jared and bellowed, 'Yo, boss. There's a hottie out here asking for you. With flowers.'

A disembodied voice shouted in return, 'Leave the poor man alone and send him through, please.'

'Amy's in the kitchen,' Trixi simpered in a sweet voice, holding back the navy curtain. 'And if there is *anything* you need, I'll be right here.'

'Thank you.' He nodded in reply, well aware that Trixi was ogling at the rear end of his fine tailored suit trousers as he squeezed past her.

Into his personal vision of what chaos must look like.

The kitchen was a mess of smeared surfaces, spilled glop in various colours, and plates and cutlery scattered everywhere.

Worse. Jared tasted sugar at the back of his throat.

He hated sugar.

The only baker he had ever met before today had been the cook at his boarding school. That lady had been middle aged, built like a sumo wrestler, and a source of constant amazement to the hormonally challenged older boys because of her expansive bosom and what looked like her triangular legs sticking out from below her sturdy tweed skirt. And, wow, could that woman swing a rolling pin!

The only person in this small, incredibly hot room was a slim, short jumping bean of a girl, in navy and white check trousers and what at one time must have been a navy apron. Tufts of brown hair escaped from the edges of a blue and white bandanna, drawing attention to an oval face with dark eyebrows and a classically curved bow of an upper lip.

Her apron, arms and trousers were splattered with white and brown blobs. Dripping blobs that matched the contents of the bowls and plates she was clearing away, at what looked like lightning speed, and the colour of Trixi's shirt.

What had Lucy got him into?

He sighed out loud. He couldn't help it.

Amy whirled round at the sound, expecting to find Trixi, who thought that any unattached man who entered Edlers was a hottie.

So far she had been wrong every time.

But not today.

She gave Jared a second look, and then a third.

This hottie qualified under the very tall, handsome businessman category.

He had expertly clipped, ultra-short dark blond hair, and the last time a man had worn shiny black shoes and a pinstripe business suit in her kitchen he had been her bank manager—and he certainly hadn't looked like this guy! The top two buttons of his pristine white shirt were undone, highlighting a deep natural tan, but he still had to be stiflingly hot under his buttoned-up cashmere suit jacket…

He definitely didn't look like a social worker or a care assistant.

And yet there was something in the way he was looking at her.

The intensity and power of this man reached out and grabbed her by the shoulders, as though he was daring her to look into his face.

His square jaw was covered in light designer stubble that extended up to thin sideburns and a faint blond moustache, and pale blue eyes focused on her below heavy brows, above a nose that had been broken more than once at its bridge.

There was something vaguely familiar about him—something she just couldn't put her finger on. Particularly around the eyes, and in the deep crease between his eyebrows.

Interesting. They must have met before somewhere.

Amy swallowed down her surprise at being caught unawares, and gave her unexpected guest a smile.

'Hello, there. Looking for me?' She gestured to one of the hard chairs arranged around her kitchen table. 'I'll be right with you, but in the meantime why don't you take a seat and tell me how I can help? And, since it is a Friday evening, how about some strudel? On the house!'

Amy dropped her icing-covered spatula into a mixing bowl, slid a white china plate towards him through the debris, then drew a long baking tray from the serving hatch.

'I'm sorry—I don't know your name. But welcome to Edlers. I'm Amy.'

She slid the fragrant warm pastry onto the plate with one hand, then lowered the tray to the table and extended her free hand towards him, her eyes locked on his. Her gaze was intense. Focused.

Jared stared at the food, then looked up into a pair of green sparkling eyes and took her hand.

It was warm, small and sticky with long, strong fingers which clamped around his. This was no limp girly hand-shake. This was the hand of a woman who cooked her own food, kneaded her own bread and washed her own dishes. Her wrists and forearms were strong and toned.

He was accustomed to shaking hands with men and women from all sides of the building trade every day of the week in his job, but this was different. A frisson of energy, a connection, sparked through that simple contact of skin on skin.

Her fingers gripped his for a second longer than necessary before releasing him, her eyes darting to his. The crease in her forehead told him that he was not the only one to have felt it.

Her eyes were not simply green. They were a kind of forest-green, spring-bud-green—the kind of captivating green which knocked the breath out of his lungs.

It was hot outside, but it had suddenly become a lot hotter in this kitchen.

Must be the heat from the ovens.

He had expected Amy Edler to be the business manager, or the finance director—not the cook! *This* was the girl Lucy had boasted about when they discussed her wedding plans? The bridesmaid who had become a rising star in the banking world before moving back to London? Surely there had to be some mistake?

Then he noticed the time on the wall clock behind her head.

Of course. Her chefs must have gone home for the evening, leaving her to clean up their mess. And she had her work cut out there.

Her attention was totally focused on him, and her head tilted slightly to one side as she waited patiently for his reply.

'Jared Shaw, Miss Edler.' He smiled back, glad to have a chance to squeeze a word in. 'Lucy's brother.'

Just for a second her gaze faltered, and a chink appeared in the façade through which he felt a faint glimmer of something unexpected. Suspicion, maybe, but also a fierce intelligence and power. It lasted only an instant. But it sent him reeling before the open-mouthed smile switched back on.

'Jared. Of *course*! Sorry—I wasn't expecting to see you until later in the week. Lucy mentioned that you might be back in town before the big day. Welcome to Edlers, just the same. It's nice to meet you at long last.'

'Likewise. And these are for you, Miss Edler.'

The pretty girl stopped moving and stared hard at the expensive bouquet of exotic bird of paradise blooms mixed with tropical foliage and sprays of yellow orchids for one second longer than he had expected, before slowly taking them from his left hand.

'Is there a problem? Don't you like them?'

Her head shot up. 'Just the opposite—they are totally gorgeous. It has just…er…been a while.' Then the sunny smile shone back at him, with a voice to match. 'That was very thoughtful of you, Jared. Thank you. And please call me Amy. I'll just put these in some water. Now, talk to me about the wedding while I finish clearing up. Lucy and Mike are going to have a blast.'

Jared straightened his back and ignored the chair, his eyes focused now on the back of her jacket as she dodged from table to sink. Had this girl truly been a banker? The few city girls he had dated were definitely not the types to get their hands or their clothing—*especially* their clothing—anything close to dirty.

'That's why I'm here. Lucy tells me that you have been working with her wedding planner to keep things on track.' He casually raised one hand. 'I'm going to be in London for a couple of days, and I would like to do whatever I can to help you with the arrangements.' He opened his arms out wide. 'It's obvious that you're busy. So you see, Miss Edler, I am completely at your disposal. Think of me as your Man Friday.'

Amy lowered the huge bouquet of stunning blossoms onto her draining board, turned slowly on one heel, and stared hard at the man standing in *her* bakery, *her* kitchen, leaning on one of *her* chairs in the home she had worked so very hard to create.

And burst out laughing.

A real belly laugh emerged from somewhere deep inside her, which made it quite impossible for her to do anything but hang onto the sink until the shaking had stopped.

When she had finished sniffing and wiping her eyes, she simply glanced in the direction of the startled blond hunk a few metres away and grinned.

'Oh, I'm sorry, but that was priceless. Rather like your face right now.'

Jared opened his mouth, pursed his lips, tugged at the double cuff of his right shirtsleeve, then the left, before shaking his head and replying, 'I'm confused. All I did was offer you some help. What was so funny?'

'You were.'

Amy dried her hands and strolled over to the table so that she was facing him.

'Lucy told me what you'd say. I didn't believe her, of course. Except…well, you've just used the precise words she said you would—right down to the "Man Friday" offer. That's all.'

There was silence for a few seconds. His fingers clenched and unclenched a few times around the back of the kitchen chair before there was an almighty sigh.

'Did my precious sister also mention that I hate to be predictable?'

Amy nodded sharply. 'She did. But I understand. You're her big brother and you want her to have the best. Nothing wrong with that. Sorry for laughing—it wasn't at you personally, just at what you said.' And then she slapped her hand over her mouth as another bout of sniggering hit her.

He shrugged. 'Perhaps I should come back tomorrow?'

Amy flapped both hands at him. 'It's been a long hot, busy day. Let's start again, shall we? How about a cold drink? I might have some juice left. Or would you prefer lemonade or water?'

'Thank you, but no. I'm still wondering what precisely you found so funny.'

'Oh, no secret. Do you ever watch those talent shows on TV? You know—the kind where people audition to show what they can do? Sing, dance, juggle monkeys?'

'I don't have time to watch much TV, but, yes, I know what you mean… What has this got to do with Lucy?'

'Last time she was in London we decided that we would both apply to be contestants on *Girls Got Talent*. She would show off her famous artistic skills, while I'd dazzle the judges by cooking up a hot soufflé on live TV. Simple, really.'

Amy strolled around the table and polished a pristine fork

on a clean corner of her apron before placing it next to the pastry on Jared's plate.

'Just because I chose to become a baker, it does not mean that I handed my brain in at the gate with my company credit card.' She smiled up at him. 'Relax, Jared. Lucy's hired a professional wedding planner. All I have to do is keep in touch every week and follow up on any questions they have. So far everything has gone very well.' Amy nodded towards his plate. 'So, now that's cleared up, why don't you enjoy your strudel? You look as though you need it. Long day?'

He paused before replying. 'Yes, actually it *has* been a long day. And I'm sure it's delicious, but I don't eat cake.'

Amy shrugged her shoulders. 'Good. Because this is not cake. This is strudel. My strudel. Which I made. Today. In this kitchen. At some silly time of the morning.'

Amy gestured towards the oven and then sat down on the corner of the table, her arms folded.

'*You* made this?' There was genuine surprise in his voice.

'Specialty of the house. And nobody leaves this kitchen without trying my strudel. Including you. Jared Shaw.'

Amy uncrossed her arms and leant forward so that her face was only inches from his. Lucy Shaw was one of the few people Amy had called to her hospital bed when she'd needed a friend. And she had no intention of letting Lucy down when it came to the simple matter of organising her wedding.

The last thing she needed was a macho brother turning up, questioning her abilities.

Even if that brother did smell of sharp citrus with a hint of leather, and looked as if he had stepped out of a photo shoot for a fashion magazine.

In another time and place she might even had said that he was gorgeous.

He was staring into her eyes now, the corners of his mouth turned up with a flicker of something which could have been amusement, but was more likely frustration that she had not agreed to hand over the wedding plan to his PA. Yet.

The next few days were going to be demanding in so many ways. Although she hated to admit it, if there *was* a problem so close to the wedding it might be helpful to have someone she could call on in an emergency. Just as long as they understood who was in charge, of course.

'I might be able to use your help on a few things,' she whispered, in her softest, most seductive tone. 'And then again, I might not.'

Her eyes ratcheted down to the pastry, then slowly, slowly slid up the front of his pristine suit jacket and back to his face.

'It all depends on what you do in the next five minutes. So what's it going to be? Jared?'

The creases at the corners of his eyes deepened, and Amy inhaled a powerful aroma of spicy masculine sweat and body spray, which was sweet even against the perfume of the fruit and nuts of her food.

She couldn't move. There was something electric in the few inches of air between them, as though powerful magnets were pulling them together.

So *this* was the famous Jared Shaw, CEO of Haywood and Shaw.

At this distance she could feel the frisson of energy and strength of the man whose property development signs were outside homes and office blocks in cities all over Britain and the East Coast of America.

And he knew it.

This was the kind of man who was accustomed to walking into a cocktail bar or a restaurant and having head waiters fawning over themselves to find him the best table.

Well, not this time, handsome!

She could stick this out longer than he could.

The bell saved him. Amy's private cellphone rang a couple of times before she dragged her eyes away from his, glanced down at the caller ID, twisted her mouth with annoyance, and stood up quickly to take the call.

Within seconds she had turned back to face him, and he instantly recognised a certain look in her eyes which brought his back even straighter.

'Yes. I can be there in twenty minutes. Thank you.'

Amy exhaled slowly, then marched to the back of the kitchen and shrugged off her long apron, revealing a short-sleeved navy blue T-shirt.

She was still drying her hands when Jared walked up.

'Do you remember the wedding planner that Lucy hired? The one with all the celebrity clients?' she asked.

There was a sharp intake of breath from the man standing ramrod-straight next to her, his back braced. He was looking horribly tall, as though he feared the worst and the wedding plan might be about to hit the fan.

It hit the fan.

'Clarissa has cancelled all her appointments and eloped to Antigua. With the bridegroom who was supposed to be walking down the aisle tomorrow morning. I'm going to her office right now to pick up Lucy's file. Want to come along?'

CHAPTER TWO

HE HAD known something like this would happen.

Worse. It was entirely his fault.

He had taken his eyes off the ball and allowed a wedding planner he had never met to run a project as important as his only sister's wedding. So what if he was in the middle of one of the biggest deals of his life in New York? Family came first.

He had promised his mother before she moved to France that he would take care of his sister.

He had let her down.

Not going to happen. Not while there was still blood in his veins. He had a brilliant PA, and a team back in New York who could be on the next flight out if they had to.

The sound of a car horn snapped Jared out of his thoughts, and he ran the fingertips of both hands through his hair, before flicking open the buttons of his suit jacket.

Suddenly he felt hot, tired, and running on empty. He went to the door to get some air. Maybe he should have eaten some of the strudel? It wouldn't have killed him. He might even have liked it. Lucy would have told him to be kinder to her friend who was offering him free food.

But there's no such thing as a free lunch, Lucy Lou.

Even if Amy Edler was not the girl he had expected.

As he turned away from the London traffic whizzing by outside, Amy jogged past him out of the shop door; her arms full of Edlers cake boxes, and nudged him in the arm before speaking.

'We're going to need serious bribery to pull this one off—and I don't mean a wad of twenties.' She nodded down the busy street. 'There's a bus that stops across the road which will have us at the wedding planner's office in fifteen minutes.'

'The last time I was on a bus,' Jared said, pulling out his cellphone, 'I was still in school. That won't be necessary.'

Amy looked up as a glossy silver-grey Rolls-Royce car glided to a smooth halt only three feet away from where they were standing. She leaned closer to him. 'Drat. A customer. And we are totally out of Sachertorte. Wait a minute—I recognise that car from somewhere!'

Jared was holding one hand up and he gestured towards the car.

'Relax. I was on my way home from the airport when I stopped by. Let me take those boxes for you, and let me introduce you to my driver, Frank…'

Jared watched in amazement as Amy literally threw the boxes at him and ran into the arms of his old friend to receive a warm bear hug. He could only stare, slack-jawed, as Amy stood on tiptoe and kissed Frank heartily on the cheek.

And *damn* if he didn't feel a tug of jealousy.

Where had that come from? He didn't do jealous. Especially not for a woman he had met only minutes earlier.

He faked calm indifference as he carefully balanced the cake boxes on one arm while he opened the boot, its shiny metal surface blocking his view of the intimate greeting.

'Amy, love. So this is where you've been hiding. Well—Edlers?' Frank shook his head and crossed his arms to scan the shopfront. 'You actually did it! Lucy should have told me.'

'You're welcome here any time—you know that, Frankie. You can have anything you can dream of eating.'

Jared closed the boot, as Amy stepped back from Frank with a beaming grin on her face, transforming her from being pretty into the kind of woman worthy of more than a second look. Even a third.

Under the fluorescent kitchen lighting he had not missed the fact that Amy was the kind of girl who looked good without make-up, but in the fading sunlight her skin appeared pale and translucent in contrast to the bright sparkling green of those amazing eyes. But it was her smile, her bright-eyed, rosy-cheeked smile, that hit him hard in the bottom of his stomach.

This version of Amy Edler was a stunner.

Something twisted inside Jared's gut and he swallowed hard. When was the last time any girl had looked at him like that with such warmth and affection? And meant it?

Come to think of it, when was the last time he had met a woman outside business? A woman like Amy Edler? Maybe if he had the time he could turn on the charm and persuade her to turn one of those smiles in his direction. Except he did not have the time. He had a week to plan his sister's wedding before he turned his back on London for good, and nothing was going to get in his way.

'I take it you two know each other, then?' Jared managed to ask casually, as he strolled over to hold the rear passenger door open for Amy.

'Who else would little Lucy call to collect her best friend from the airport? Rent-a-cab? Not likely, mate. Only the best for this lady.' Then his expression changed, and Frank reached out and held Amy by both arms. 'You look great, girl. Gorgeous as ever. How are you feeling?'

As Jared watched, the smile faltered on Amy's lips, before she relaxed. 'Fine—I'm fine. Never better.' Her words were softer, lower, as though she was protecting Frank from some unpleasant truth.

Frank gave a sharp nod and turned back to Jared.

'I know a great new Italian place, mate. How about we all catch up over dinner?'

Amy laughed out loud and spoke before Jared had a chance to answer.

'Not a chance, Frankie. The wedding planner Lucy hired has done a runner. Eloped. Taken off with the fiancé of one of her clients.' Amy lifted and then dropped both her arms. 'I had the first call, but we need to get over there fast, before the other bridezillas find out.'

Frank hissed, and jumped back from the pavement towards the driver's door. 'Jump in. You too, boss. Fast as you like. I know the address, but we're going to have to get a move on before the news breaks. I know a shortcut.'

Amy was halfway into the car when she suddenly jumped back onto the pavement, turning at the same time and colliding with Jared's hard, muscular body.

Jared reacted instantly, grabbing her by the waist. His fingers expanded to take in her tiny waist and the curve of her ribcage. The woman hidden beneath the baggy navy working clothes was muscular and warm, and it made absolute sense for him to hold her tighter in his embrace, both of his arms encircling the slim body.

'It's okay. I've got you.'

Amy blinked and opened her mouth to speak, then closed it again as her eyes locked onto his.

The portion of Jared's brain responsible for sensible thought and blood pressure forgot that he was standing on a public London street, with Friday night pedestrians only a few feet away, and his breathing changed to compensate for the thundering in his heart.

His body reacted to the warm tiny woman pressed against his chest, her hands flat against his business shirt. The smell of her body and her clothing—warm vanilla, sweet spices and bread—combined with the sound of her breathing loud in his ears, blocking out the thundering traffic and street noise.

Time expanded until his arms slowly slid away from her waist and he took one step back. He drew himself to his feet, holding her steady, and she released him and stepped to one side.

Amy lifted one leg, then the other, inspecting the fabric of her trousers.

'Sorry about that. But I've got chocolate icing on my trousers. And this is a nice car…'

The two men stood and stared at her in silence for a second, before Frank dared to comment.

'I've had a lot worse on that leather. Dig out the picnic blanket, mate, and then let's get going.'

'How well do you know this wedding planner?' Jared asked as soon as they were moving and he had regained use of his lungs and his brain.

'Clarissa?' Amy answered. 'I only met her the last time Lucy was in London. Her assistant Elspeth was in charge of making the actual arrangements. I know a few girls who have used Clarissa, and they all sing her praises. That's why I'm not worried. It's only seven days to the wedding, Jared. Everything will have been booked and confirmed weeks if not months ago.'

He conceded it was possible with a nod. 'Maybe, but there is no harm in checking. Especially now. I don't want to call Lucy until I know whether there is a problem.'

'I agree with you on that.' Amy swallowed and tried to appear casual by looking out of the window before going on. 'So, what can I do to convince you that I don't need your help and am perfectly capable of sorting out any last-minute problems on my own?'

Jared considered for a moment before replying. 'I need to be sure that this Clarissa hasn't missed anything in her rush to elope with some other girl's boyfriend. For me, that means going through the master checklist for the project, right down to times and places.'

'Ah. Is that all?' Amy laughed, and stared into his face with her mouth half open. 'I'm beginning to understand. You cannot stand the idea that any person besides yourself and your team is even remotely capable of running a project. Am I right?'

There was some suppressed sniggering from the front of the car, which at that moment turned sharply into a tight bend, sliding Jared along the slippery leather towards Amy, who was safe on her blanket.

His hand grabbed onto her leg to steady him, and was rewarded with a smudge of something sticky between its fingers.

And the sensation that his world had been rocked on its foundation.

He felt dizzy. Light headed. He should have eaten that strudel. That was it. Nothing to do with the slim muscular thigh he had just been touching. Must be jet lag.

'Seatbelt?' she murmured, shaking her head. 'Seatbelt would be good.'

He clicked on the belt, pretending to look out of the window.

Unfortunately for him at that moment he saw the reflection of Amy in the glass.

She was digging inside the bag on her knee with one hand, while the other stripped back the bandanna covering her hair. In one smooth movement her head dropped back, her eyes closed, and her fingers combed through her head of boy-short glossy brown layers.

It was the most sensual thing he had seen in a long time, and the fact that it was natural and completely relaxed made it even more remarkable.

The dark brown hair contrasted with Amy's smooth clear skin, shining in the June sunlight streaming through the car window. She had been at university at the same time as Lucy, he thought, so she had to be late twenties...

Her head flicked up as she laughed about something with Frank, as though they had been mates for years.

Why did he find that so annoying? Frank was free to act

as a chauffeur as and when he liked when Jared wasn't in town—which was the usual case. He couldn't have spent any more than a week in London in the last six months. Why *shouldn't* he drive Lucy and her friends? That was what he had asked him to do, wasn't it? But why hadn't Frank mentioned Amy before? And what was the great secret they'd been talking about when she'd hugged him like that?

A police siren sounded to their right, and Jared turned as Amy flicked out her tongue to tantalisingly lick off the smudge of icing at the corner of her mouth.

She noticed him looking her way. Or had she noticed the sudden increase in temperature in the gap between them? Frank should take a look at the air conditioning in this car…

Time for him to take charge.

'So, how do I get to see this famous wedding plan?'

Amy sighed out loud. 'That is not going to be easy!' She turned in her seat before going on. 'Each of Clarissa's clients has their own personal file. Everything and anything linked to that particular wedding is inside that pink box. Rule one is that the box should never leave her office, on pain of death. I'm hoping sweet treats will persuade Elspeth to change her mind about that, while she copes with the fall-out from Clarissa's sudden exit.'

Jared pushed his full lower lip forward and gently inclined his head.

'Devious. I like it. And I thought the way to a *man's* heart was through his stomach!'

'Oh, it works for ladies too! I suspect we may not be the only ones burning a path to that office to salvage wedding plans. The brides will burn me at the stake for bringing carbs, but their mothers will love it.'

'Clearly. I can see now where I've been going wrong all these years. I should have been buttering up my girlfriends with sugar and cakes.'

'Definitely.'

Amy glanced out of the window as Frank slowed to a stop. Cars were double and triple-parked down the narrow street outside the wedding planner's office. Some more abandoned than parked.

'Here we are. And it looks like I'm going to need that cake. Best stay in the car, boys. This is a dangerous assignment, but someone has to do it. I'm going in.'

Jared stared across Amy to see what could be so dangerous.

They had pulled up outside a row of Victorian terraced houses, once the homes of the middle classes, now used as businesses and hotels all over the city.

This particular house was distinguished from its neighbours by a tasteless pink plaque with the word "Clarissa" in black and gold six-inch-high letters.

And by the cluster of women around the entrance.

Sleek, shiny women. Of all ages. Jostling to get into the house.

The kind of women who were accustomed to the January sales and came supplied with sharp elbows and stiletto heels. And his shin pads were back in New York. This was more than dangerous—this could be lethal!

Jared instinctively touched Amy on the arm as she removed her seatbelt.

'No way are you giving *those* ladies extra sugar. You'd never make it back alive.'

Amy collapsed back into the luxurious seat and glared at the increasingly noisy crowd. Several more cars had pulled up behind them, ready to discharge extra troops.

'You may have a point. Frank? Any ideas?'

'Retreat to a safe point and come back Monday, when these girls have gone home to complain to their hairdressers?'

'Not possible.' Jared interrupted before Amy could reply. 'Lucy is due to be married in seven days? Monday will not do. You two stay here. I'll see how far I can get.'

This time it was Amy who grabbed Jared's arm, as he tugged on the cuffs of his shirt.

'Hold on, macho hero. Those girls would eat *you* alive. You do know that it's always the bloke's fault, don't you? This bridegroom who stole Clarissa from them is clearly to blame for the whole thing. You'd have to be pregnant and barefoot to get to the front of *that* queue!'

Jared sat back and pursed his lips together for a few seconds as he looked at Amy, from her flat comfortable shoes to the top of her head, before nodding slowly.

'Pregnant and barefoot. Hmm. That's not a bad idea. It might just work…'

Amy caught the tone in Jared's voice, and watched as he patted the picnic blanket she was sitting on before speaking.

'I'm almost frightened to ask,' she said, watching him closely.

'Frank? Do you have any cushions in the back?' Jared asked, totally ignoring her comment.

'Of course, mate.'

'Excellent. Miss Edler—I do realise that we have only just met, but we are about to become proud expectant parents. Won't that be nice?'

She stared at him with wide-eyed horror as she realised what his idea was.

'You wouldn't?'

The man sitting next to her simply turned towards her and gave a wide smile, raising his eyebrows.

It was the first time he had smiled since they'd met—and, oh, yes, she could see why any girl in a fifty metre radius would instantly agree to anything he suggested.

Amy closed her eyes. She had promised Lucy she would do everything she could to help with the wedding while her mother recovered from the 'flu.

And of course there was that other reason it had to be a huge success…

This might be the first wedding cake Amy had ever made,

but it was not going to be the last. Clarissa had already contacted her about other weddings later in the year, and she knew Lucy had been telling all her London friends. She already had orders for eight more chocolate special cakes—but only if this wedding was the success she desperately wanted for Lucy and Mike.

She needed that business.

She needed her friends to have a wonderful day.

She needed that wedding plan.

Which was why she suddenly heard herself asking, 'How many cushions? One or two?'

Jared took his time climbing out of one side of the car and making his way around the rear to open the passenger door for Amy, so that she could start her award winning performance.

He made a show of making a slight bow, so she accepted his hand as if she was stepping out in evening dress onto the red carpet at a film premiere. Only on this occasion she was wearing navy check trousers splattered with icing, and a stained extra-large navy T-shirt stretched over two pillows and a picnic blanket. But she was still determined to give the role her all.

It wasn't her fault that her performance required Jared to wrap one arm protectively around where her middle should be, which somehow distracted her so much that she was swept up the steps before she knew it. Thereby missing her own big entrance.

Jared helped Amy stagger through into a narrow corridor packed with anxious and crying women who had jumped to their feet as one, each female fighting to make her voice heard, competing in decibels and speed to get attention. Any attention.

The noise was deafening.

Amy squeezed Jared's hand—a signal to reposition the pillow, which was starting to bulge over her trousers—before stretching up to whisper in his ear.

'Let's make a deal. If I can persuade Elspeth to give me the box, then I *will* allow you to help with the wedding. But only on one condition. You do the work yourself. Not your PA, not your events planner, not your brilliant admin team. *You*. Or is the great Jared Shaw scared of getting his hands dirty?'

She looked up at him with the sweetest, most adoring, open-mouthed smile, complete with fluttering eyelashes for the benefit of the onlookers.

'Do we have a deal? Squeeze once for yes, and twice for no.'

Jared tightened his grip on Amy's waist. The way back to the car was already blocked by a formidable-looking older woman and a younger weeping girl.

There was no backing out.

He squeezed. Once.

Still clutching Jared's hand, Amy dragged him towards the flustered-looking receptionist's desk. The pillows and picnic blanket had created a surprisingly effective eight-month baby bump.

'Hi. I've heard about Clarissa's unplanned holiday.' Amy addressed the girl behind the desk, glancing around the room, taking in the tears and the emotional tension, until every other woman stopped talking.

'My fiancé and I have our wedding *next weekend*.' She looked at the stunned Jared and gave him her most adoring smile. 'This is our last chance before little Jarella is born, so I hope you understand that I have an urgent appointment in—' she glanced at her watch '—three minutes.'

Before the receptionist could answer, Amy leant backwards and shuffled up to the office door, drawing a red-faced Jared with her. She knocked once, did not wait for an answer, flung open the door, and then closed it behind them.

A slim, middle-aged woman in a tight pink bouclé suit was crouched down low, her elbows resting on a pink desk. Her head was in her hands, and the desk was covered with yellow sticky notes. A loose telephone lead trailed from her finger.

Disconnected. There was a bottle of cream sherry and a small glass by her hand. And not much sherry left in the bottle.

'Hello, Elspeth. Remember me?'

'You can do this,' Amy said, looking into the terrified eyes of Clarissa's personal assistant, who was still nibbling on buttery flaky pastry courtesy of Edlers Bakery. 'You can take over these weddings. You were doing most of the work yourself, weren't you?'

Fragments of pastry scattered onto the paperwork as the older woman's hand paused in mid-air. 'Yes, I suppose so. Clarissa was so busy entertaining clients she relied on me to make the actual bookings and talk to the suppliers—like yourself. Boring things like that.'

'Not boring,' Amy insisted. 'Important. Especially to the brides-to-be out there with their mothers.'

Amy sat down next to the terrified woman on a pale pink sofa, and tried to ignore the fact that the icing blobs on the back of her trousers would probably ruin the pink silk.

'You want to be a wedding planner, don't you? Was that a nod? Right!' She reached across and took shaking but beautifully manicured hands in her still-sticky, grubby paw. 'This is your chance. You have the power to give those girls the weddings they have always dreamed of. *You* created the files. You did that. Not Clarissa. You. Now all you have to do is to convince your clients that it's business as usual. The plans are in place and on track. What do you say?'

'Well, I don't know. I've only been working here two years. Until then Clarissa organised everything herself. I'll need to go through each box…' The panic came back into her eyes as she gasped. 'The Shaw-Gerard wedding! You're making the cake! That's next weekend, and I haven't even looked at the file. The box is still here. What if…?' There was terror in the unspoken words as she reached for the box, only to find that Amy had got there first.

'Don't you worry about that. I'm going to take Lucy's file home with me. I'll go through the plan myself, check the details, and meet you back here during the week. Okay?'

'Well, I don't know. I mean, Clarissa is pretty strict about the files not leaving the office without the client's permission.' She paused, gulped, and looked into Amy's face.

'That's not a problem. Mr Shaw here is the person who signed the contract—so he is the client, after all.'

Elspeth looked up at Jared, who was guarding the door, and gave a faint smile. 'Well, that's true. We have met before. How about four p.m. Thursday?'

Amy smiled back. 'Done. And you can *do* this. Seriously. You can. You're the new wedding planner. Ready to face the music? Head up, shoulders back. Show them who is in charge here.'

She leapt to her feet, helped pull the woman up from the sofa, and watched as she tugged at her pink pencil skirt. With one single nod, Amy took a firm grip on Lucy's pink-flowered box file, clutched it to her chest, flung open the door with her other hand, and beamed a smile to the cluster of women who leapt to their feet and started crowding in at the door.

Jared seized the opportunity to take back control of the situation, and he rested his arm lightly on Amy's back before calling back casually to the terrified-looking PA.

'Thank you so much! We have every confidence in you. See you on Thursday!'

Amy was so startled that she looked up at him in awe. And in that moment her heart skipped a beat. No wonder Lucy boasted that her brother could charm the birds from the trees.

He was grinning the kind of grin toothpaste manufacturers would kill for, his white teeth contrasting with his blue eyes against a light natural tan. His mouth creased up at the corners, creating what could almost pass as dimples. If hard-nosed CEOs were allowed to have dimples. She could almost hear the women around her swoon as his gaze fell on the lucky girls at the front of the pack.

She didn't blame them.

Jared Shaw truly was gorgeous.

And then he did it.

He casually turned his spotlight smile on her, bent his head a few inches, and kissed her. On the brow. Just a light pressure of hot lips on her skin, before he dropped his arm a few inches lower and stepped forward.

Her knees turned to jelly.

She was caught in his embrace with nowhere for her spare arm to go except around his middle, against the fine linen cloth that covered an impressively taut muscular lower back.

There was nothing for it but to breathe in the aroma that only a man who had been on a hot pavement followed by her hot kitchen at the end of a long day travelling could generate. It was sweet, spicy, and intoxicating.

For a second—just for one, precious moment—Amy luxuriated in the illusion that they were trying to create and made herself believe that Jared *was* her fiancé, and she *was* carrying his baby—that his relaxed lover's kiss had been real and for her.

Dangerous. Way too dangerous.

She forced herself to glance up at that handsome strong face, and the icy-cold realisation that this was a man who could have any woman he wanted sent her tumbling back to earth from dreamland.

That dream was for other women. That chance had been snatched away from her. She was an idiot for daring to think otherwise. And an even bigger idiot for thinking back to that moment when they'd been getting into the car. The feeling of his warm shirt under the palms of her hands. The beating chest that lay beneath.

What was she *doing*?

This was Lucy's big brother. In town for a few days for his sister's wedding. That was all.

And with that positive thought Amy squeezed into his

waist a little closer, wrapped her fingers firmly onto his belt, and flashed a smile up into his face.

Luckily he took it as part of her star performance, gave a quick nod and, smiling at the closest cluster of ladies, the unlikely pair slowly shuffled as convincingly as they could down the corridor, with the pretend baby bump leading the way.

Jared gave one quick glance back at the building, before launching himself into the Rolls-Royce through the door Frank was holding open. He sighed out loud in relief to have escaped unscathed, as he collapsed back in his seat.

'That was horrendous. Why would someone actually *want* to be a wedding planner? I mean, why? What chance has that poor girl got with those women at her throat? What did you call them?'

'Bridezillas. Elspeth is quite capable of handling the work—but she has my telephone number if she needs it. And I have Lucy's box.' Amy waved it triumphantly towards Frank, before pulling the squashed cushions out from beneath her top. 'Sorry, Jarella. What's next?'

It was Jared who answered.

'Apart from ten hours' sleep? Coffee, telephones, a photocopier and a computer. It appears that I have a wedding to organise.'

CHAPTER THREE

'THAT'S ten strawberry tarts, twelve apple strudel, and six fresh cream chocolate éclairs. Well, that should keep you going, girls! Just pop back if you need more.'

Amy passed the emergency order to the two waitresses from the French pavement café down the road, and held open the shop door. Their jovial teenage chatter echoed around the warm room and blended with the traffic noise from the busy London street on the other side of the glass this lovely Saturday morning.

Both girls were dressed in the kind of pretty printed cotton dresses with thin spaghetti straps that she used to wear every summer in her old life. Sunlight flooded through the pristine glass windows and reflected back from the cream walls onto the warm terracotta floor tiles. It would be heaven to simply strip off her chef's jacket and spend the rest of the day in a tiny top. Except, of course, she had thrown or given away all her tankinis and strappy dresses.

Anything that would have revealed the scarring which stretched down the centre of her chest.

The palm of her hand pressed down on the raised ridge of skin below her T-shirt and jacket. The plastic surgeon in Chicago had suggested that she should think of it as a medal.

A souvenir for a survivor.

And she *was* a survivor. At least he had got that bit right.

A familiar lump thickened in Amy's throat as she looked back into the shop area, bustling with customers and bright chatter.

This was her home now, and her sanctuary. Her dream of making Edlers the place she had known as a girl had become a reality. This was where she wanted to spend the rest of her life. Safe, secure, running her own business, with her friends in the community around her.

This was where she could offer a child a loving home—just as the Edler family had done for her when her own parents died.

And that was worth every scrap of energy in her body.

Trixi sidled up next to her and flung an arm around her shoulder.

'Two more hot chefs at the back door, boss, panting for their orders. No sign of that blond bloke from yesterday yet. Is he likely to turn up today?'

'Oh, yes. He'll turn up. At least, I hope he will.'

The sound of trance dance music hit Jared like a wall as he stepped through the curtain into Amy's kitchen. It was almost noon on a Saturday morning, the sun was shining, and the beat was making the walls and floor throb. Just like his head.

If only he hadn't decided to lie down on the sofa after dinner he could have been working through the photocopy of the wedding plan back in his air-conditioned apartment at that very second.

In control and in his own space. Which was precisely how he liked it.

Instead of which he would have to go down on bended knee and beg this girl to take pity and let him off the hook. He knew his strengths. Coming up with a comprehensive schedule of works for a building project was one thing— planning a wedding was something else.

If you wanted a job done, you hired a professional.

Through his sunglasses he could make out that Amy was alone. She appeared to be jogging between two long tables covered with trays and boxes, furiously writing on printed sheets on a clipboard. Where were all the other chefs?

'Morning,' he offered with a smile. No response. 'Good morning,' he bellowed, standing only feet away from Amy. At that precise moment the teenage girl he remembered as Trixi appeared from a door at the other end of the room and turned the volume down on the stereo.

Amy's head shot up, and she gave him the kind of smile that creased the corners of her mouth and made a direct hit in his solar plexus.

'No need to shout. I'm right here. And good morning to you, Mr Shaw. I expected to see you at the crack of dawn.'

There was a certain gentle warmth in her voice, as though she might actually be pleased to see him again. Maybe the day was not completely lost after all.

'Sorry about that. My body clock hasn't re-set yet.'

'You don't need to apologise,' she replied with a shrug. 'Yesterday was quite a day.'

The muscles of his face relaxed a little. This woman was a saint! The hard fluorescent lighting in the room focused the shadows of her high cheekbones and pale skin. In another time, on another day, Jared thought, it might have been fun to show this woman some sunshine. Perhaps a picnic, or a boat trip down the Thames?

With a bit of luck she might even remove some of those layers of clothing. His linen shirt was already starting to cling to his back, despite the heavy-duty air-conditioning unit clattering away very noisily in the corner. She had to be roasting under that high-neck T-shirt.

Amy waved her clipboard in his direction. 'Saturday happens to be my busiest day, so there's not a lot of time for chatter while I get the orders prepped. I appreciate the apology, but I know you only came here to collect the pink box.'

He opened his mouth to speak, but snapped it closed again as Amy tapped her pen several times against her chin before grinning at him.

'I have decided that there could be one or two *small* details on the wedding plan which you could check for me. If you think you can manage it?' she said.

Jared pursed his lips and sighed loudly. 'You do know that I have zero experience in anything wedding-related, don't you? I could even be a liability!'

'No, you won't. Just think of it as another project to plan. You'll be fine!'

His grimace must have been the answer Amy needed, and she gestured towards the small circular table furthest from the ovens and the work area.

'You'll find what you need on the table over there. I've already cross-referenced the details on the master checklist to a printout of names and addresses. Not all of the suppliers are open on Saturdays, so I focused on the names I recognised, and I've written notes on everyone I could speak to in person at this time of the morning.'

'And...?' Jared tried to remember that *he* was supposed to be taking charge. *So much for his cunning plan. Amy Edler was already way ahead of him*!

She decided to put him out of his misery.

'Relax, Jared. So far all the items I've checked are still on schedule. You can breathe again.' She nodded her head towards the table and curled her lips. 'There are two names we need to talk to as soon as possible. I started with the hotel, but they have a celebrity wedding this morning, so their events planner had already left for the church, to make sure everything went smoothly.'

She spotted the expression on Jared's face and immediately tried to calm him. 'Don't panic. According to the manager, the Shaw-Gerard wedding is booked and confirmed for next Saturday. But I don't have any details, so that needs to be checked out—I suggest Monday morning. Everyone is going to be run ragged today.'

He snorted. 'You've got that right. Okay. You're busy. I have the rest of the day. Why don't you leave me to start work on the rest? I have my laptop, two phones, and transport if needed. What do you say?' Jared looked up, half expecting an instant rebuff, but it never came.

'I say fine. There's a fax machine and a photocopier upstairs in my flat if it becomes too noisy. This place is going to get rather hectic in the next couple of hours!'

Jared blinked at Amy several times. He simply could not keep up!

'When do the other bakers start work? Or have they already left for the day?'

The crease between Amy's brows tightened. 'Other bakers?' And then the penny dropped. 'Oh, I see what you mean. Sorry to disappoint you, but there is only one baker at Edlers, and you're looking at her. Trixi and her pal handle the shop counter, but I'm on my own in the kitchen.'

She tilted her head to look at him, paused, and then nodded with a wide grin. 'You thought there was a whole brigade of professional bakers working here, didn't you?'

'You…are the only baker?' Jared waved in the direction of the curtain leading to the shop area, the astonishment in his voice only too apparent. 'You made all that food your-self?'

Amy held up both her hands and wiggled their fingers up and down. 'With my very own, very wrinkly hands.'

'That's impressive. And all the more reason why I should take on this extra work and leave you to do what you clearly do best. My admin team is used to event planning; they'd be happy to help.'

'Maybe. But not if you have questions about details this late in the day. And I thought we discussed that last night? That, sir, was not the deal.'

He bit his lower lip. *Busted.*

She took pity on him and pointed towards the small table.

'Sit. I drink coffee. Espresso. But there is tea and water if you want it. The bathroom is through there, and Trixi is going to be too busy to bother you. And there is always cake if you get the nibbles.'

'Thanks; I'll stick with the coffee. Anything else, boss?'

She made a face and tried not to smile, tapping her clipboard instead as a distraction. 'The second person I couldn't get hold of is the photographer, who is not answering the number Clarissa has. He's probably out working on another wedding, but his office is supposed to be open on Saturdays. He's on page two of the list.'

'No problem. Leave it to me.'

'Oh, actually, there is one more thing.' Amy pressed her lips together, fighting back laughter, and pretended to study her list. 'You can take your sunglasses off now.'

For the next hour or so Jared juggled two mobile phones, a landline, and a dodgy wireless connection on his laptop—all set against the background clatter and chatter of a room which at times was more like a railway station than a working kitchen.

Just as he checked off an item on what seemed like a never-ending list, the back door would open and a stream of youngsters wearing chefs' overalls carrying the logos of famous restaurants from all over the city would saunter in, to collect trays of food for their dinner service.

What amazed him was that not only did Amy know each of them by their first name, but she also looked happy to stop what she was doing and go over their order and discuss the food. And laugh. Nattering in French, German, Italian or Spanish, as needed. A couple of times she even dived into the shop area to select another of the round chocolate cakes, or wrap another loaf to increase the order.

It seemed relentless.

And then there was the baking. Every time he looked up Amy was pulling tray after tray of sweet smelling food from the ovens.

If there was ever a one-woman show, he was watching it. And he had thought *his* office was busy.

It was almost a surprise when he looked up to find her wandering over to his table with a tray of coffee and some tiny pastries. Jared leapt to his feet and took the tray from her hands as she collapsed down into a hard chair and dropped her head back, eyes closed.

'Is it always like this?' he asked.

She flicked open her green eyes and looked at him across the table. 'I've had to work harder than I have ever done in my life to build this business. There are some excellent bakers in this city who have been training for years. I have to offer something special. And I've only been open two years. That's not a long time in this world.' She laughed. 'I carry the battle scars to show for it.' Amy stretched out her arms so that Jared could see the burn marks from wrist to elbow.

He gasped. 'That's horrendous. From the ovens?'

'Hot baking sheets. My uncle Walter calls them campaign medals. All part of the job. I knew what I was getting myself into before I started.' Then she laughed again, and picked up a fragment of flaky pastry filled with cinnamon-scented cream, before passing the plate to Jared. 'Besides, do you think all the top chefs have time to make their own strudel?'

'What about all those round chocolate cakes that have been going out? Surely they can make those?'

She put down her coffee cup and glared at him. 'Are you referring to my Sachertorte, Mr Shaw? That is a secret recipe handed down through generations of the Edler family. Direct from Vienna, you know.' Her hands wrapped around the coffee cup she was focused on. 'I should warn you. There is a definite risk involved in allowing that cake past your lips.'

'A risk?' He smiled back, suddenly losing all interest in the contents of Lucy's pink box.

'Oh, yes. I have several customers who claim that they are addicted to it. No other chocolate cake will do! I would hate to get you hooked on the best. How would you cope when you go back to New York?'

'You don't deliver?'

'Only within a ten-mile radius of where you are sitting.'

'Well, I can see that could be a problem. Although...'

She tilted her head towards him and smiled as her eyebrows lifted.

Jared stared her right back. 'I take risks for a living, Miss Edler. Part of my job is looking for the next challenge.' He paused, his eyes still locked on hers, before speaking in a low voice. 'Bring it on.'

The crinkles at the corners of her eyes smiled back. And the background noise in the room around them was blocked out by the sound of his heartbeat. He felt as though the rest of the planet did not exist. That they were floating in space. Just the two of them. Separated from the world. Together. How had that happened?

Then a very real and loud human voice broke the glass wall.

'Amy! Time to head upstairs. The gals are here. See ya later!'

She turned her head away from Jared to reply to Trixi with an, 'Okay.'

The spell was broken.

'Sorry, but my flat will be out of bounds for the next hour or so. Trixi is using my shower.' Amy gathered up the coffee cups and poured a glass of cold water for them both, her eyes focused on anything apart from Jared. 'Back to work. Would you mind talking me through the list while I make a few extra loaves? That would be great!'

Jared nodded in reply and instinctively moved his chair

across, next to the table where Amy was working, suddenly keen to be close to this woman. He stretched out his long denim clad legs, and was about to ask her what table decorations were when something heavy and loud fell onto the floor above their head. Jared the builder wondered if the floorboards were original, and if they were likely to have Trixi falling through to join them at any minute.

A voice called out from the ether. 'I'm okay.'

Jared looked up at Amy, who was shaking her head.

'Now I am intrigued. *Why* is the lovely Trixi using your bathroom?'

Amy sighed and carried on working the ball of dough.

'Trixi lives at home, and the shower in their flat hasn't been working for weeks. Their landlord always finds some sort of excuse as to why it can't be repaired.'

Jared nodded. 'I know the type only too well. He's stalling. It's never going to happen.'

'Correct.' Amy nodded too. 'The problem is Trixi's mum is a single parent in a wheelchair, and it's one of the few disabled access flats to be found. He knows that. So they have to either lump it or move out. And he knows they can't afford to do that.'

Amy sighed out loud and started thumping the life out of the dough on her board, punching and teasing it.

'Do you know that girl has to wash her mother's back each day with only a flannel and a bowl of hot water? She needs a shower. The poor woman only has a bath once a week at the Saturday clinic. Trixi is worried sick. She can't even plan to go to college. Not with that responsibility.'

'What's she doing about it?'

'Working two jobs to raise the money. Filling out forms. Making calls to charities and organisations for the disabled. Going to the local authority. She's too independent to ask for a handout from me, but I've been working with a group who might be able to help. It makes me so angry!'

Jared pointed at the board, which was almost bouncing.

'Whatever you're making, it surrendered two bouts ago.'

Amy laughed. 'The more energy you put in, the better the bread. It needs another five minutes. Haven't you tried it? Best stress release in the world! Come on—I've seen that frown on your face for the last ten minutes. And you're grinding your teeth. Bad sign.'

'Me? What a pity I'm not dressed for it.'

She glanced down at his sky-blue shirt and jeans and smothered a sigh of appreciation.

'I have a manly apron you can use. You shall not be ashamed.'

True to her word, Amy wiped her hands off before reaching for a navy and white long butcher's apron from a peg on the wall. She held it out with two fingers towards Jared.

'You're serious? You want me to bash that sticky stuff?'

'I'll show you how. You can wash your hands over there. Soap, nailbrush. Your manicurist will never know. It can be our little secret.'

'I don't think so.'

She walked around the table and waved the apron in front of him.

'The sooner the dough is kneaded, the sooner we can get working on Lucy's plan. I only have a few more loaves to finish. And from the looks of it you need to thump someone more than me. Simply imagine your least favourite person and let them have it.'

'Anyone?'

'How about the lovely Clarissa, who is at this precise moment lying on a tropical beach next to a long cool drink with a parasol in it.'

Jared got the picture and clenched his teeth. It had cost him a fortune to take care of his teeth, and now he had started grinding them again.

He accepted the apron and dropped it over his head, daring Amy to laugh. She didn't laugh, but gave him a nod of approval instead.

'Very smart. You almost look the part. The sink is over there. Then get ready to have some fun.'

She was interrupted by her telephone and, excusing herself, took off to the back door to take the call.

Fun? This was supposed to be *fun*?

Jared had tried every way he could, but the mess of flour and water was sticking to his fingers in big lumps, the amount on the board was getting smaller, and Amy was still on the telephone.

He stared down at the paste between his fingers and growled at it. There was no way a piece of dough was going to beat him, so he pressed his fingers into it, willing the fragments to reform into the shiny smooth balls Amy had made previously.

He heard a noise to one side, and stood up as Amy strolled next to him and stared down.

One of her hands was covering her mouth, and she had to be biting the inside of her lip to stop herself from laughing.

'It's okay; I know it's a mess. Don't burst a blood vessel.'

Her hand dropped away, and she grinned and shrugged her shoulders.

'I *had* intended to give you a lesson before you started. Flour. Lots of extra flour. And the heel of your hand—not the fingers. Let's get rid of this and start again.'

In an instant the mess was wiped away and replaced with the final two pieces of sweet-smelling fresh dough.

'Stand next to me and watch for a while. You'll soon get the hang of it.'

Jared was pressed shoulder to shoulder with Amy as she sifted flour onto the board and the dough, then raised her right hand, pointing to the part next to her wrist. She pressed the palm and heel of her hand into the dough, pressing it flatter, stretching it at the same time away from her.

'The trick is to push down and forward at the same time.

Every time you stretch the dough the gluten in the flour is worked a little more. Here. Your turn.'

Amy flipped the dough back on itself and took Jared's left hand, guiding it onto the dough, meshing her own fingers with his as she pressed down and forward.

When she tried to lift her fingers away Jared pressed his right hand down on top of hers, moving their fingers together on the warm, soft dough. She turned her head to ask what he was doing. Only his body moved a precious, special inch closer to hers, and she inhaled the heady aroma of expensive aftershave, freshly laundered shirts and Jared. Spicy. Hot.

She made the mistake of lifting her gaze to his eyes.

And was lost.

He wasn't just looking at her. He was staring. His eyes were locked on hers like laser tracking devices. Intense. Below the blond brows his eyes were not pale blue, more sky-blue, with flecks of amber and navy at the centre of the dark, dark pupil.

It was like looking into the ocean from the side of a boat and seeing only your own reflection, because what lay beneath was so deep, so dark, that the light could not penetrate. And yet she had to keep looking.

He was mesmerising.

She had to gulp down air in the heat of that stare.

His sharply cut upper lip moved only a fraction as he whispered, 'You noticed I was left-handed?'

She nodded, unable to trust her voice at that moment.

'Most people miss that.'

His right hand came up, and its forefinger gently pressed against her cheek, as though to wipe away a smudge of flour.

She had to fight not to close her eyes at the pleasure of that simple touch of skin on skin. So tender. So loving it was almost painful.

'Am I getting the hang of it?' Jared asked, and both of them knew he wasn't talking about his cooking skills.

'No. Hopeless. And I have a rush job. Sorry. Maybe another time.'

She stepped to one side, desperate to escape temptation in an apron, and grabbed the dough ball, working if furiously as she talked.

'One of my regulars is hosting a birthday tea this afternoon, and she's had a disaster. Oh, could you pass me that flour-shaker, please? Thank you.'

'Disaster?' Jared asked, his arms outstretched on the table. The only place they would be safe.

'One of her girls split up with her boyfriend last night, and consoled herself by eating one entire birthday cake and most of the child-sized treats when everyone else in the house was asleep. I need to conjure up mini-cakes and a chocolate button special for twenty little girls in the next two hours. So—rush job.' She glanced across at her audience. 'Hello? Anyone home?'

He was staring, transfixed, at the spongy sticky mess which was being transformed before his eyes into a perfect roll of smooth, springy dough.

'That. Is. Magic.'

She kept kneading. 'Magic. I like that. Much better than technical words like gluten.'

She stopped kneading so that she could get his attention.

'May I make a suggestion?'

'This is your kitchen.'

She nodded to the pink box and the checklist and clipboard Jared had deserted to play at being a baker. 'I have my hands full here. It would be fantastic if you could visit that photographer who is refusing to answer his phone, and find out what is happening in person. Would you mind?'

'Done. And let me supply the coffee this time? Seeing as you provided a free lesson and floor show.'

'That would be excellent. Thanks. Now, shoo—go! She turned back to her work, flapping her hands in his direction. 'And keep smiling. You may need to, partner!'

CHAPTER FOUR

IT WAS late in the afternoon before Jared wandered back across the busy road towards Edlers Bakery, carrying his precious load of coffees.

And he wasn't smiling.

The wedding photographer had been offered a chance to work on a wildlife documentary in Mongolia about wild camels.

Yes, he *had* taken a booking for the Shaw-Gerard wedding in June, and, yes, he had asked another photographer he knew to take the job, so that he could head out to Mongolia. Hadn't Clarissa told them?

At least the weather was glorious. Jared had decided to walk back to the bakery to ease the tension from his shoulders. Maybe Amy had more of that bread dough he could pound?

He had been wrong to slot Amy Edler into the bored-banker-with-a-hobby pigeonhole. Badly wrong. Beneath that sinewy little body was a woman with real passion for what she did. He had seen it that morning with her customers, and he knew talent when he saw it.

How did she cope on her own? Lucy claimed that *he* was a workaholic! Maybe Amy crashed later in the day—although he doubted it.

Nevertheless, he had promised the girl coffee, and her first real break of the day.

Jared turned the corner and watched the cluster of customers jostling in and out of Edlers, their jovial chatter drowned out by the sound of the traffic.

The builder in him could not resist thinking of what he could do with that shopfront. A modern entrance would transform the place and probably double the turnover. Especially on a sunny Saturday, when most of the local residents had to walk past her front door to get to the main shopping area.

He could always suggest it. After all, that sort of investment would be a drop in the ocean.

Except, of course, that would double the workload for Amy. From what he had seen today the girl was doing the work of at least two bakers, as well as running the business. She would need more staff. And what about parking?

He wandered into the delivery bay behind the bakery.

And stopped dead in his tracks.

Parked in the paved yard outside the back door of Edlers Bakery was the oldest, rustiest, sorriest excuse for a small white delivery van that he had ever seen in his life. *Ever*. The noise coming from under its bonnet told him everything he needed to know about the state of the engine. The clouds of dark sooty smoke spluttering out from the exhaust explained the rest.

And sitting in the driver's seat was a red-faced Amy Edler.

He swallowed down his horror and sauntered up to the half-open driver's window. He tapped politely on the glass, pretending not to notice that the whole van was now shaking.

'Coffee, madam? And perhaps a new engine?'

Amy hissed something in a language he did not understand, which brought Jared's eyebrows together as he fought not to laugh.

'Thank you,' she replied, trying to force the gear lever into first, 'for the coffee. But not right now. There are thirty iced cupcakes, and a full birthday special which need to be six streets away in the next half-hour, or a certain eight-year-old will be very disappointed. And the staff will be on medication. Please have some coffee yourself—I'll get mine later.'

At that point the van shuddered again, then gave up completely and stopped.

'How much later?'

Amy slapped her hand hard on the dashboard.

'Hannah came with the shop. And she passed her MOT test ten months ago!'

She turned the key a couple of times in the ignition, her face growing redder and redder in heat and frustration.

'Come on, old girl—don't let me down now! Especially not in front of a man.'

Jared swallowed down a joke about women and cars, and glanced at Amy's face. She was serious. This was her business, and she needed to make this delivery.

'Ahem. You've killed her. You and the cylinder head gasket, the blown exhaust and the ruined clutch. The transmission and electrics are probably shot too.'

She paused, unclipped her seatbelt, and turned to stare at him in silence.

He prepared himself for a cutting remark along the lines of *How would you know?*—which would mean explaining how his after-school homework had been working for Frank in the grottiest garage repair shop in London.

Only the remark never came.

'Seriously?'

He nodded once. Slowly.

'Are you saying that she is not going to run?'

He nodded again.

Amy's head dropped to the steering wheel, her eyes closed, and she gave a little whimper.

Jared lifted his own head and thought of something positive to say in a hurry, to cheer her up. 'You could always sell the numberplate and buy a decent little runabout. EDL1 has to be rare.'

Her head shot up. 'Sell the *what*? Are you *mad*?' she

shrieked. 'This is Hannah—the original Edler delivery van. I am *not* selling my van or my numberplate! Now, do you have any sensible suggestions, Mr Shaw, before I call a black cab?'

'Only one. My four-wheel drive is parked around the corner. It has a cavernous boot which I seldom use.' He let that sink in, before closing the deal. 'We could be there and back before the coffee goes cold.'

Her large green eyes flicked back to the dashboard, then to her watch, before she nodded.

'This one time—and only because it's a Saturday and the world has gone mad, and I need to make this delivery. Yes, thank you, that would be very kind.'

'No problem.' He went for the door handle to help Amy out. Only the handle was broken as well, and he had to simply watch as Amy stroked the leather and spoke to the van in a gentle voice.

'He didn't mean it, Hannah. I'll be back soon to make you feel better.'

Jared stepped away from the madness, shook his head, and popped the coffee into the kitchen before slipping past Trixi and onto the street.

As he waited to dodge the traffic, Jared flipped open his mobile phone.

'Frank, mate, I need to pick your brains. Yeah, I know. Hysterical. Who would I go to for a new delivery van these days? Top notch. Amy Edler needs a replacement in a hurry. Oh, and Frank? There's a lovely lady about your age who is dying to meet you. Name of Hannah.'

'Ashcroft Grove. It's the third turning on the right.'

'Ashcroft?' Jared shuffled in the driver's seat as though the hot leather was burning through the fabric of his jeans. 'There used to be a children's home on Ashcroft.'

'There still is. That's where we're going now!'

He glanced across at her before replying in a low voice, 'The children's home?'

'Absolutely.' Amy shook her head and opened her eyes wide. 'I'm amazed you've remembered that, Jared. Has Haywood and Shaw been working in the area?'

'I'm far more interested in your connection to that place. There used to be about thirty kids in that home. You can't cater for all that lot on your own!'

'I don't.' Amy gestured to the trays in the back of the car. 'At the moment Nell has about twenty girls, from seven to seventeen, and today is definitely a one off. Just a chance for a shy eight-year-old to have a normal birthday tea with her friends from school. I'm glad to be able to help out.'

'Do you mean Nell Waters? Nell was in charge of the place years ago, but I heard that she was thinking of retirement.'

'Not likely.' Amy broke into a broad smile as she looked out into the tree lined street and propped her feet up on the dashboard. 'Nell is one of my best friends around here. It was her idea to hold an after-school club in my kitchen on Friday afternoons, and the girls love it.' She lowered her voice to a conspiratorial whisper. 'Don't tell anyone, but so do I. Even if they do leave the place in a mess. It's worth it.'

Jared paused, and pretended to be checking the traffic before replying. 'Will Nell be here today, at this party?'

Amy glanced at her watch. 'No, we've missed her. But she did love the cakes the girls iced yesterday.'

'Aha. So the kitchen decoration yesterday evening was not all your own work?'

'Not entirely.' Her voice softened, her eyes welled with tears. 'They're great girls. All they want is the chance to show another human being what they are capable of achieving without being judged differently from anyone else. It's not much to ask.'

Jared turned slowly into Ashcroft Grove before speaking

again, his eyes firmly fixed on the narrow street. 'Lucy's never mentioned that you were in a children's home.'

Amy dropped her feet from the dashboard, and focused on something very fascinating on the other side of her window.

'That's because I didn't tell her. I haven't told anyone, Jared.'

Her eyebrows moved closer together. She was tense and anxious, the pain on her face only too evident. 'So how did *you* know? Did you work out on your own that I was in a home? Is it that obvious?'

Jared stayed focused on the road ahead. 'To me it is. I could hear it in your voice when you talked about the girls and being judged.'

Amy sighed out loud and inspected her fingernails.

'I only spent six months in Ashcroft before Maria Edler applied to adopt me, but I'll never forget it.'

'How old were you when you lost your parents?'

Amy shuffled forward in her seat and straightened her back. 'Twelve. But let's not talk about that. I'm far more interested in your plans for the wedding—you know, the plans which aren't on Clarissa's list.'

Jared got the message to drop the subject and immediately lifted the tone in his voice. He knew only too well how hard it was to talk about being taken into care. 'Anything specific?'

'Well, I would like to know what the honorary father of the bride speech sounds like—and then of course I have a personal interest in your presents for the two bridesmaids.' She paused and waggled both her eyebrows at him. 'And then there's the big one.'

'I hate to ask…'

'I do hope that you've been practising your ballroom dancing!'

Jared snorted a chuckle before replying. 'Oh, no, you don't catch me out like that. I checked the list very carefully this morning—no dance band or orchestra. I am totally off the hook.'

Amy patted her upper lip with one finger.

'But we *have* booked a DJ capable of playing records? Am I right?'

Jared drummed his fingers on the steering wheel and pursed his lips. 'She would, wouldn't she? Just to humiliate me a little further.'

Amy nodded very slowly as Jared gritted his teeth in exasperation and slowed down to park outside a large brick house, where dozens of children were racing up and down the grass, playing ball games.

'I knew I should have paid Mike to elope with Lucy to some sunny beach somewhere. Do you have any more pleasant surprises for me this afternoon, Miss Edler?'

Amy looked out just as some of the children recognised her and started running towards the gate.

'Guaranteed. Starting right now. You're carrying the cake. And it has to survive the frontline scouts.'

Over two hours later Jared was driving down the side streets of London, breathing slowly and trying to lower his blood pressure.

'Please tell me you don't have to do that every week! The little horrors practically ripped the buns out of my hands! I had no idea baking could be so dangerous.'

'Ah. To be fair, I think they were already high on white sugar and artificial colours from the jelly and ice cream before we got there. Thank you for the support, by the way. There are clearly some advantages to being taller than six feet. At least the birthday cake made it as far as the table—and they loved you playing with them.'

'No problem. The bruises will fade in a few weeks.'

She looked at his knees and hissed.

'A good dry cleaner *might* be able to get the strawberry sauce out. And you did get your very own fake eye patch for playing pirates! Can't say fairer than that. Sorry you missed out on the chocolate buttons cake.'

Jared chuckled and shook his head before replying. 'Let's

call it a new experience. Speaking of food—is there any chance we can find some before getting back to work? My body clock is telling me that I missed lunch.'

'After all those delicious party nibbles? The very idea.' She laughed out loud. 'It will have to be a snack since I am going out for dinner this evening. How does smoked salmon and scrambled egg on toasted brioche sound?'

'It sounds like heaven! Simply tell me where to drive and your wish is my command.'

'Well, I know this charming little bakery. Terribly exclusive! Oh, don't look so worried—I *can* cook. And, since I live there, I'm much less likely to run off like our wedding planner and our photographer.'

'Ah.' Now it was his turn to laugh. 'Well, at least the bread will be good.' He paused and checked the rearview mirror. 'So, who is the lucky man?'

'Um?'

'It's Saturday night. You deserve to relax with him.'

'Actually, I'm meeting Nell at a charity function to raise funds to keep the children's home going. Let's just say that I'm between boyfriends at the moment. How about you, Jared?' she asked, trying her best to sound casual while looking out of the window. 'Do you have a hot date for tonight?'

Jared paused, stunned by what she had just said. 'Me? No. Not tonight. Ah.' He looked through the front windscreen, grateful for the chance to change the subject. 'I recognise this street.'

Amy laughed out loud. 'You should do—it's not five minutes' walk from my bakery. You must have driven down here several times.'

'Well, in that case can you spare a few minutes, Miss Edler? I would appreciate your expert opinion on a new bistro we've been working on.' He shrugged and glanced towards his passenger. 'It's an important new client and we're only three weeks from handing the place over. I collected the keys this morning.'

'I think I can manage that,' Amy replied, but then looked down at the dusting of flour and the havoc sticky eight-year-old hands could create still clinging to her clothes. 'I'm not exactly dressed for smart restaurants. They are more used to seeing me at the tradesman's entrance.'

Jared smiled and scanned her clothing a little longer then necessary. 'You'll be fine. I bought this site eight months ago, but we only completed the fitting last month. I know Lucy is in charge of interior design, but I'd like to check how the work is going for myself.'

'Ah. Now I understand. You have to rely on your site manager to carry out your instructions instead of supervising them yourself. I can see how that might be a problem for you!'

He laughed out loud. 'Guilty as charged. Haywood and Shaw have a lot of work at the moment, and Lucy is keen to complete the decorating before she starts her honeymoon.' Jared's voice trailed off as he turned the car into the space in front of a detached two-storey building.

Or what would have been a space, if it had not been for the overloaded skips, building debris and piles of broken wood and plastic sacks which blocked the car park.

They sat in silence, both staring out at the building site.

A large placard nailed to a post told the world that this was 'A Haywood and Shaw Development of Specialist Retail and Food Outlets'.

It was Amy who decided to take the plunge.

'I think we should go inside and take a look.'

Jared exhaled. Very slowly. Before nodding, once.

He said nothing as he helped her down from the car, but the thunderous look on his face said volumes. Amy said a silent prayer that the place would be gorgeous. For both their sakes.

Amy stepped back as Jared turned a key in the heavy wooden door, but she knew that he had already peered through the slits in the plastic sheeting on the tall windows to see the chaos on the other side.

Her prayers were not answered.

It was not gorgeous inside. The Haywood and Shaw tradesmen had gone home for the weekend, leaving behind a huge mess.

Jared closed the double doors behind them, and they stood side by side in the wide entrance. The tiled and parquet flooring had been covered with dustsheets, piled with battered tins of varnish and paint. Brushes, rags and cleaning materials were piled into plastic buckets. Two large ladders blocked the way down the corridor.

Amy glanced behind her to see Jared staring at the high ceiling, one hand thrust into a pocket, his shoulders high with tension.

Amy followed Jared's eyes to the ceiling, where an elaborate and clearly original plaster cornice and matching circle had been picked out in brown. It was a pale brown, but it was definitely brown.

'What colour did Lucy say that she wanted?'

'Last time I spoke to the painter it was ivory. Gold and dark cream plasterwork. That was a week ago. A month ago it was porcelain blue. A month before that oyster.'

'Ah. Well, the walls are definitely ivory. But I would describe that colour as more of a beige brown than a dark cream. I think this may need a telephone call. Mind if I have a look around?'

He nodded before flicking open his cellphone. 'Feel free. The flooring should all be down.'

Drat. Lucy always boasted about how her darling brother spoilt her all the time. Maybe that had come back to bite him.

High curved archways led into the main dining area, in front of the long tall windows which separated the room from the trees outside. Jared was right. The shell of the building and the walls and flooring were solid, and would look stunning once the paintwork was complete.

The restaurant space was already gorgeous and full of light, even with the windows half blocked. It only needed curtains, carpets and furniture to make it wonderful.

And then she turned the corner and stopped dead in her tracks.

This was the restaurant kitchen to end all kitchens.

It was a huge room. At least as big as the reception area. And clean. There were only three dirty tea beakers draining on the sink to indicate that anyone had been in here at all. It was a palace of stainless steel and easy-to-clean surfaces.

She stepped forward, suddenly eager to open cupboards and drawers. Top quality appliances. A walk-in larder. Two dishwashers. And the *ovens*! Two serving hatches... She sighed out loud in delight.

A beam of sunlight shone through a gap in the black covering on what looked like the back door of the kitchen.

She could not resist it; she pulled away the tape from the end door, turned the key, and stepped out onto sandstone flagstones warmed by the sun.

A lovely modern conservatory extension had been built onto the long, wide dining area to create a stunning room with direct access to the landscaped gardens. A professional had been at work here, and the brightly coloured flowerbeds and lawn arrangement had been superbly designed around a large patio.

She imagined what this would look like bustling with garden furniture for customers to eat outside on a June day like today, and smiled in the sunshine. And it would make a safe play area for children—away from the traffic on the busy street but close enough for their parents to watch them in comfort.

It was the only thing missing at Edlers. She would have loved a garden for the girls in the after-school club to play in and enjoy, without worrying about knocking over council ornaments or public planting in the park.

It was a wonderful space.

The daughter she had not met yet would love it here.

There was noise behind her, and Amy turned her back on the garden to see the view into the dining room. Looking through the ivory-coloured high arches, with the sun on her neck, she was instantly transported back in time to another room so like this one it was frightening.

In that room dark red blinds had shielded customers from the sunlight that escaped from under the matching awning outside the coffee shop. Crystal drop chandeliers and round glass globes had lit the booths along the edges of the room, their intimate glow reflecting back from cream floor tiles, dark polished wood and one long mirrored wall.

She could almost see the business men reading their newspapers over their mocha coffee as the gentle chatter of the crowded room swirled around them, and ladies lingering over their exquisite chocolate and nut gateaux as their lovers gazed fondly into their eyes, and the young man in the corner who had been there for hours, scribbling notes at a round marble-topped table. Nobody had moved him on.

The air had been filled with the bittersweet aroma of freshly ground coffee and chocolate, of buttery pastry and a faint tang of cigarette smoke from the patrons.

It had been the perfect Viennese coffee shop. And, best of all, she had been there with her precious adoptive grandparents.

Amy inhaled deeply before smiling away the prick of tears. She hadn't thought of that holiday for months.

The sound of footsteps made her turn back to Jared, who had decided to laugh rather than hit something.

'My darling sister has changed her mind again, and asked the guys to hold back on any more decorating until she can see what the colour looks like in natural light. The clean-up teams are due in Monday. It might be okay after all.'

He came up to Amy, who had not moved from her spot, and looked into her face. 'Well, something has made you smile. First impressions?'

She looked up towards him, her face cracked open with a grin, and grabbed at his sleeve in excitement. 'This is a magical place. I love the kitchen and the extension. It's the most amazing, fantastic… Oh, I *love* it!'

She sighed in happiness as she released him, and sat down with her back against the sun-warmed stone. 'May I please sit here for a minute longer?'

'Well, I did ask for first impressions. Thank you, Amy. The building still belongs to me at the moment, so be my guest. Stay there as long as you need. I'm glad you like it!'

'Like it? Get down here, you—and not another word.'

Amy looked up at him, then tugged at his sleeve until he slid down the wall, laughing, and sat next to her, shoulder to shoulder. She wriggled into a more comfortable spot.

'Ten years ago I spent a wonderful two weeks with my adopted family in Austria. Salzburg was wonderful, but when we went to Vienna?' She sighed in pleasure. 'Oh, Vienna changed my life. After Vienna I knew why the Edler family spent so many hours each day in their bakery, dreaming of owning their own coffee shop. It all made perfect sense.'

'Is that why you bought their old bakery?'

She nodded. 'Maria Edler was Walter Edler's sister, and every Saturday she and I used to travel down to the bakery together so that she could do his accounts while I played in the kitchen. It was brilliant fun. I only hope they live long enough to see *me* open a Viennese coffee shop and invite them to the grand opening. Wouldn't that be something for them to remember?' Her voice trailed away to a whisper. 'Maybe one day.'

There was no reply, but she sensed him reaching out and lacing his long strong fingers between hers as though it was the most natural thing to do in the world.

Her head dropped back against the wall and she swallowed hard, not trusting her voice at that moment. She would not cry, or dare look at his hand or his face.

Focus—focus on something else.

Slowly the noise of the traffic slipped away until she could hear birdsong. A robin bobbed down from a branch. Blackbirds. A song thrush sang high in an apple tree in the next garden. A breeze brought them the perfume of the roses trained against the wall only yards from where they were sitting, and mixed with the scent of the man whose arm was touching hers.

How could she not imagine what it would be like to live here, work here, make this house the new Edler coffee house and bakery? And, best of all, a garden where her children could play. It would be perfect.

Perhaps one day she *could* have a place like this.

Jared shifted next to her, and her happy dream crashed back to reality and a kitchen full of work waiting for her. Amy flicked her eyes open and slowly slid her fingers away from Jared's. The sun was moving behind the beech trees.

One dream too many.

'I should get back. But thank you for my five minutes in the sun. Your client is a very lucky person, Jared. And this will be a perfect bistro—although I would recommend a more conventional seating arrangement.' She grinned as she pushed herself up with the palms of her hands, and then yelped in pain.

'What is it?' Jared asked, taken aback.

'Only a splinter—it's nothing.' She blinked away the pricking tears of pain.

'Here—give it to me. Come on, show!'

Jared snatched her hand and stared at the palm. A colourful expletive exploded from his mouth before he remembered that he was not alone, and looked back at her shocked face, his neck flushed an attractive shade of red.

'I knew I should have come here first this morning!' He shook his head. 'I am *so* sorry, Amy.'

She smiled in reply. 'I think I may live. Do you have any

tweezers I could borrow?' Then she laughed out loud at the look on his face. 'Stupid question. I can pull it out later, back at the bakery. What?'

Jared was shaking his head. 'This is my problem. And I used to be something of an expert in splinters. I know it may not look like it now, but Lucy used to climb trees for a hobby. If you can stop wriggling for a minute I'll press it out. Ready?'

He looked into her face as she took a breath and nodded once.

She pressed back against the wall and prepared herself for pain. What she wasn't prepared for was the sensation of his fingertip running down the centre of her palm.

She gasped, and he winced, thinking he had hurt her.

'Sorry. Almost got it. There. All done.'

And then he did it. He rubbed her skin with his soft thumb, pressing hard and then softly, the sensation running down her arm to the place where her loving and sensitive heart used to be—until it had been ripped out two years earlier.

And now she was looking at someone who was capable of ripping it out all over again, as he stroked her hand, sending delicious shivers of pleasure up her arm.

Why hadn't she gone back to work? Stupid! This wasn't where she wanted to be. Not now. Not any more.

Amy slid her hand away from between Jared's fingers, and pretended to look for other splinters, her eyes focused on her own skin—anywhere but on this living, breathing man, so close that she could smell his Jared smell.

It was overpowering. Too intense, too tempting.

She was going back to work. Back to her own sanctuary. She could do that. She could freeze him out to protect herself until she had finished the cake and this wedding was over. She was good at that. She had to protect herself from the pain of being rejected by this man. She just *had* to.

She glanced at her watch, pushed herself back from the

wall, and was on her feet in seconds, smoothing down her apron. 'Thank you for showing me the bistro—and this wonderful garden.'

Then, without thinking or hesitating, she stood on tiptoe and pressed her lips for a fraction of a second against the side of his cheek.

'And most of all thank you for bringing back such happy memories.'

Jared watched her go back inside in stunned silence, amazed by what she had just done. 'You're welcome. Come back any time you like. Any time at all.'

CHAPTER FIVE

JARED sauntered casually off the red carpet and into the ball-room of the central London hotel, the camera flashguns lighting up his back. He tugged at the cuffs of his evening shirt. He might be the youngest sponsor of the event, but this was the one time a year he was willing to put his Armani tux on show for the press and wear his heart on his sleeve.

There was only one person who could have persuaded him to come back to London.

Nell Waters.

The same Nell Waters who ran the children's home he had been to with Amy that very afternoon. He hadn't been able to believe it when Amy had mentioned her name. How could she have known that this was the same Nell Waters who had been a social worker twenty years ago, given responsibility for the Shaw household?

Nell Waters had been the one person Jared had feared and trusted all at the same time. He had known that one slip, one sign of a dirty house or a missed day of school, and the whole charade he had created would have disintegrated.

Of course she'd known that his mother had worked three jobs to keep them going, using every contact and old friend she had ever met to find work.

She'd had to.

Their father had been in prison, their every penny sucked away by his greed and ambition for drugs and gambling.

It had been Nell's job to check that Lucy and Jared were well cared for. She had supported them every way she could, and eventually conceded that the teenage Jared was probably doing a better job of taking care of his little sister than most of the mothers on her patch.

His education had been another matter.

The constant worry about whether he was going to be able to collect Lucy from school on time, and get the washing done, and cook the dinner, combined with the weary battle to keep himself and Lucy clean and well fed, had left him exhausted at school during the day.

And then his mother had gone down with gastric 'flu for a week, and he'd known the game was up. He hadn't been able to keep up with his homework and look after his family. So the brightest boy in the class had started slipping further and further behind, until it had come as no surprise to the teachers when he'd decided to leave school as soon as he was able and start work for Frank Richards, who ran a garage repair shop below their flat.

Both of them had known that he could do more than wash and service cars, but it had been his way of making sure that his sister did not come home to an empty house.

Nell had never let them down.

She had worked hard to make sure the Shaw family had been given every grant and benefit she could find to help a family who were trying so hard to stay together. It would have been easier for her to have taken Lucy and Jared into separate foster care rather than keep them together, but she'd stuck with them. She'd trusted that Jared and his mother would not let Lucy down. And she had been right. He had worked and worked to make sure there was always food on the table.

It was through Nell Waters that he'd got his first job in the building trade.

And here was the lady herself, greeting the sixty or so especially invited guests at the door in person, same as always.

He took the wind out of her sails by raising the back of a plump hand to his lips. 'Good evening, Miss Waters. May I say that you look even more lovely every time I see you?'

He was rewarded by a soft kiss on the cheek.

'Fibber! But, my, you still scrub up nicely, Jared Shaw. And thanks again for your support. This is a fabulous venue.'

'It's my pleasure. What's this I hear about retirement? Some terrible rumour—put about, no doubt, by the government officials you terrorise on a daily basis?'

'Nope. I don't need to tell you that things haven't got any better, Jared. In some areas it's worse than I've ever known it. It needs someone younger and fitter to pull together the one hundred and one different government and private charities and give children the help they need. Time for me to hand the reins to someone more used to the world of technology.'

She looked coquettishly over the top of her spectacles at him. 'Someone like you, for example? Um? Interested in a change of direction?'

'What? You have to be kidding, Nell. Can you imagine *me* running those endless committees, knowing kids are still crying out for help? I would be tearing my hair out. What's left of it, that is.'

Nell ruffled his cropped hair.

'There. My last outrageous act. A clear sign of madness. And you, young man, would be fantastic in the job.' She took his hand and held it firm. 'Will you think about it? We need you.'

His brows came together. 'You're serious?'

'Very. But now is not the time or place. Come and talk to me next week and we can go through the job in more detail. Go and enjoy the party! See you later.' And with that she released his hand to move on to the cluster of new arrivals who had packed the room behind him.

Jared stepped to one side and tried to bring his breathing back down to a level where he could control it. Go back into that hell? See in other children's eyes the pain and horror of not knowing how they were going to wash and dry clothes for the next day, or find food for lunch?

How could Nell even *suggest* that to him? Even if he had the time—which he didn't—he would be no good to them. As of next week he would be leaving London for good. This truly was the end of his road here.

And as for trusting other people to get the job done? Forget it. It had taken him years to build up a team in New York that he could leave in the office for four days and be confident that work would be done to his standard.

Today's fiasco at the bistro had only shown him, yet again, what could happen if you took your eyes off the ball and relied on other people to take responsibility. How could he do that with so many different groups and interested parties? It would be a logistical nightmare. Worse. He would be working with the people who were present at this function tonight!

He glanced around the gilt high-ceilinged ballroom. Politicians, charity workers, journalists. The kind of people he worked with only when absolutely necessary.

And a very, very pretty girl.

Amy Edler. Only not the hard working baker version of Amy he had spent most of the day with.

This Amy was dressed in a cocktail dress. Midnight-blue. Sleeveless, high collar tied behind her neck with a ribbon. And a low-cut back. Totally hot.

Jared had seen enough French couture dresses and bought enough for Lucy on his credit card to know the real thing when he saw it.

She had spectacular arms and shoulders. Maybe there was some benefit to kneading dough after all.

The dress fitted her perfectly, its fabric draped close to her waist and then flaring out over slim hips to just above the knees.

Sheer black stockings covered long, slim but muscular legs. High heels. Silk shoes.

Tonight Amy Edler was every bit the young female corporate mover and shaker he had seen in parties all over the world. Tonight she looked like the girl Lucy had described from their university days. Efficient. Brilliant.

Only he knew the real Amy. The woman who had taken a famous bakery and transformed it into something spectacular. Doing what she loved to do—her passion. On her own terms.

When had he last met a woman like that? Not often. Maybe never. Oh, he had met plenty of glossy-haired girls with Mensa level IQs who had claimed they were doing what they truly loved. But so few people knew what they wanted in their twenties.

He had.

Amy Edler had.

Maybe that was why he connected with the tiny woman he was looking at now.

They were different from other people.

Her life force, her energy, sparkled like the jewels in the bracelet on her wrist. She was effervescent, hot, and so attractive he had to fight down the fizz of testosterone that clenched the muscles under his dress shirt and set his heart racing.

Just at the sight of her.

Jared watched Amy chatting away to the other guests. He heard her speaking and replying to questions in French and what sounded like Russian. Of course. She had taken a degree in Modern Languages.

How had he ever imagined that Lucy had made a terrible mistake when she'd chosen a baker as her bridesmaid? Mike's sister he could understand. Bella was lovely, talented, a chatty and attractive journalist and the sister Lucy had always longed for. But Amy Edler? Amy was a mystery. They had only met in their last year at university, when Lucy had started dating Mike Gerard. In fact he had almost forgotten the name until Lucy had mentioned it over dinner one evening.

He hadn't pushed it. His sister was entitled to choose her own bridesmaids.

He headed for the bar, anxious not to make a fool of himself, ogling the woman in the midnight-blue dress, but she strolled across through to the other room, totally confident and completely at ease in this group of policy makers, government officials and charity workers. It was the kind of ease which came from an expensive education and university.

He had worked hard to give Lucy that opportunity, and she had loved every minute of it. Even his mother had been impressed with how the little blonde girl at a new school, away from her old friends, had blossomed into a lovely teenager and a confident, beautiful woman with straight As and a first-class honours degree from a famous university under her belt.

It was an education designed to open doors. And it had.

He loved his sister, and was the first to admit that she had achieved her success by working as hard as he had to make it happen. And yet he did wonder sometimes how things would have turned out for them all if he had *not* left school at sixteen to work his way back to something like their old lifestyle. Maybe. And then again maybe not. Maybe his father had given him the edge, the pressure he had needed.

Past history.

He picked up a glass of sparkling water and turned back to the cluster of sponsors who were getting ready to attack the sumptuous food. At the same moment Amy smiled at one of the organisers and waltzed off, leaving Jared to stare after her. And at the low back of her dress.

Whoa.

Food? Now, that was an idea. And he started searching the room for Nell Waters. Who just happened to be setting up the auction.

* * *

'Ladies and gentlemen—the next item to be auctioned is a master class for you budding chefs out there. I'm sure you have all heard of the world-famous Edlers Bakery, located right here in London? Well, this is special. The highest bidder will receive a personal cookery lesson from the head baker in that very kitchen. Let's start with fifty pounds. Thank you.'

Amy leant back in her chair in the front row and tried to breathe normally, her head rock-solid and facing the stage, watching Nell move from bidder to bidder around the room.

Why had she agreed to this? Nell had only suggested it ten minutes before the auction started, and somehow she had agreed to sell her time and expertise to a complete stranger.

What had she been thinking?

The bidding was already at one hundred pounds when a distinctive and familiar voice rang out from the side of the room.

'One thousand pounds.'

Every head in the room turned to see who had made such an outrageous bid.

It was Jared, of course.

He was wearing a dinner suit that had clearly been made for him, and he looked like a male fashion model. His eyes were locked onto her face as though she was the only person in the room for him, and in that one single glance she saw satisfied delight, amusement, and—yes—straightforward, open desire.

No pretence. No disguise.

Gorgeous did not come close, and her treacherous heart skipped a couple of beats as he acknowledged her response.

Time stilled as she stood there, silently watching his chest rise and fall, the muscles taut under the stretched shirt fabric. As she gazed at that handsome stubbly face, and the seriously seductive full lips, something twisted below her waist. Her heart kicked hard, and she began to sweat.

Cold and then hot shivers had her clutching the chair for support.

It could be the 'flu. Only she'd been fine two minutes ago. Before she'd clapped eyes on Jared Shaw in his finery.

Which left the other possibility. Which was simply crazy.

Oh, no. You weren't allowed to reach the grand old age of twenty-eight and have a passionate crush on your friend's brother. That was teenager territory. She could *not* have fallen for Jared Shaw. She just couldn't! That would be a seriously bad idea. He was Lucy's brother! And they would be at the same wedding in a few days. Especially when that brother lived and worked thousands of miles away and was only in London for a few days.

No. That idea had to go out of the window. Now. Today. This minute.

Stupid girl. Look at him. He was the kind of man she'd used to flirt with at City cocktail parties. Tall, slim, fit, a perfect specimen—and, oh, such bad, bad news even then. And now? She had no chance.

The hotel air-conditioning kicked in, and an ice-cold blast of reality and cool air hit Amy square between the eyes. She physically recoiled with the shock.

She lifted her hand from the chair and straightened. Well, she didn't need to worry about that. There was no way Jared Shaw would be interested in *her*.

Damn Jared for proving in one single look that she had been totally wrong with every single pathetic excuse for how she had felt sitting next to him in that garden.

What had she told herself two years ago? That part of her life was over with. Done. No man would ever find her attractive again. Nothing had changed since then, and it was no different now.

Perfect men did not waste their time with girls like her. Damaged goods.

Lucy had booked two places at the wedding for Jared Shaw and his guest. No doubt there was some lovely, perfect lady flying in for the wedding, who would hang on this man's arm and dance the night away in his arms.

Not her. This man belonged to some other girl.

Well, it had been a nice dream while it lasted.

What exactly was he bidding for? A cooking lesson? Or time spent alone with her, one to one? Why would he be interested in *her*?

He raised both hands and gave her a stunning smile, displaying a set of perfect white teeth, before tossing off a casual shrug and walking away into the crowd of applauding guests at the top table, shaking hands as he went with the same local government officials she had been complaining about that afternoon.

Amy could only stare in amazement as Jared smiled for the press and the photographers.

And every person in the room saw Jared walk slowly towards her and kiss the back of her hand, giving her a private wink, before accepting his applause from the other guests and Nell.

'And the Master Class goes to Jared Shaw, of Haywood and Shaw, who we would like to thank for sponsoring tonight's event. Mr Jared Shaw, ladies and gentlemen.'

'Well, you did say that you hated being predictable!'

'So I did.'

Amy moved closer and bumped Jared gently in the shoulder.

'Why didn't you tell me that you would be here tonight? I've just spent the last five minutes listening to Nell Waters singing your praises. Apparently you have many talents—most of them clearly well hidden!'

'Was the shock too great for you?'

'Oh, I think I'll live. But you don't get away that easily. Come on. Spill. How do you know Nell?'

Jared looked over Amy's shoulder towards where Nell was still talking to her guests.

'When Lucy and I were kids Nell was the social worker

who helped us to get settled in her part of the city—she even wangled me my first job in the building trade!'

'Amazing! Lucy's never mentioned her.'

'She was way too young to remember, and we only lived in the area for a few months. Although…' He sighed. 'There is one thing I regret.'

'Oh? Please go on. This should be good.'

He was focused completely on her now, those blue eyes laser-bright. 'If we had only lived around Ashcroft a little longer Nell might have introduced me to a certain little girl before she became Amy Edler.'

Amy tried not to smile back and failed, well aware that both her neck and her cheeks were flaring red in hot embarrassment.

'You didn't miss much. But it is strange to think that we could have passed each other on the street all those years ago. I love Nell, and from the sound of it she made quite an impression on *you*!'

He shook his head and smiled, so that the creases at the corners of his eyes crinkled in acceptance. 'My company supports a lot of charities, but this is the only lady who somehow manages to charm me into turning up in person.'

'Ah. So you *are* susceptible to ladies' charms?'

'It has been known. Although some of Nell's *guests* are a challenge. Do you see that man stuffing himself with prawns? Pinstripe suit, old school tie?' Jared gestured with his water glass towards a portly elderly man with thin grey hair and a matching grey suit, who had been hogging the buffet table for at least fifteen minutes.

'The one with the huge plate of food? Got it. Do you know him?'

'He was headmaster of the private school I attended. On my last day he took great delight in telling me that there was no room in his school for the son of a criminal and I would amount to nothing.'

'Ouch! That was cruel. Shall I bar him from the bakery? I could, you know. No strudel of mine shall pass his lips.'

'Thank you for the offer, but it's not worth it. You know what they say. Success is the best revenge.'

'I have heard that, but you are smirking a little too much.' Amy looked into his face and smiled before lowering her voice. 'Come on—what did you do? Buy the school and turn it into a night-club?'

He turned away from the buffet table and grinned. 'Something very childish and silly. They demolished the old school a few years ago, but before it closed I drove there from London in a hot red Lamborghini and parked in the headmaster's space, just for the hell of it. Then I gave a thirty-minute speech about the value of experience over formal education in the modern world, before taking the sixth form out to the pub. He was livid. It was a reckless thing to do, but, boy, it felt good.'

'A red Lamborghini!' Amy laughed out loud, 'I would have loved to have seen that.' She glanced back over her shoulder. 'Does he know you are paying for the food and drink tonight? Shall I be naughty and tell him?'

'The naughty Miss Edler? Um. Now, that's an interesting thought. Do you have any other ways of demonstrating this naughty streak?'

'I punish men by making them knead bread, and then telling them how useless they are. Oh, I forgot. Already done that one.'

'Well, I was hoping that you could help me out with a technical problem that I've been having.'

'A problem? You? Surely not!'

'Oh, it's very serious.' He leant closer. 'Do you know the Noodles and Strudels food chain in the U.S.? Yes? Well, they have just become one of my biggest clients. My office has been inundated with samples for the last month. Only, seeing you in the kitchen this morning made me realise that I truly do not have a sweet tooth in my head.'

'That is serious.' Amy nodded sagely as a cluster of businessmen in suits passed by.

'You can imagine how much damage a thing like this could do to my reputation if word got out. As a businessman, I recognise when I need professional help.'

She pushed her lips forward before replying, 'Always a good idea.'

'I was almost ready to give up, and then—' he flicked a manicured fingernail at the card he was holding up between two fingers '—imagine my surprise to find that a certain Miss Amy Edler of the world-famous Edlers Bakery was offering a personal baking lesson to the highest bidder. How could I resist?'

'You have paid one thousand pounds so that I can teach you how to recognise good strudel?'

'Not at all. I have just donated an extra thousand pounds to a charity I happen to care about, and I will have the pleasure of your company all to myself.'

'Well, I take that as a compliment, kind sir!'

'You will keep your end of the deal. I know that.'

'Yes, I dare say I will. Of course I didn't say when the lesson would be taking place. I'll have to get back to you on that, Mr Shaw. Right now I need to catch up with Nell and say goodnight. It has been a very long day.'

'Then may I have the pleasure of escorting you home, Miss Edler? Perhaps we could discuss our business arrangement on the way?'

Amy looked into his smiling face and realised that there was nothing in this world that she would like better.

Jared presented a dinner jacket-clad arm for Amy to wrap her own arm around, just as she glanced over his shoulder.

'By all means, Mr Shaw. Except I think someone is trying to get your attention.'

'Jared Shaw! Thought I saw you!'

A rotund, middle-aged man, with greying sideburns and a lively open smile, walked up to Jared, and they exchanged a hearty handshake that seemed to Amy's eyes to be far more than a simple professional greeting. The cluster of smartly dressed men and women gathered around the bar parted to give them space.

And then she looked a little closer, and her eyes widened.

The man with his arm around Jared's shoulder was Bill Brooks. The Texan owner of Noodles and Strudels Worldwide.

Her frown dissolved into a smile of disbelief. Well, he *had* told her that he had an important new client. Pity he had forgotten to mention that they were friends! No wonder his office had been inundated with pastries.

As though a hidden sensor in the back of Jared's head had detected her presence, his smile turned her way, and her disobedient heart tightened as the spotlight of that smile illuminated her life. Her world.

One of Jared's arms was extended, and she drifted close enough to take the older man's hand.

'Bill, I'd like to introduce you to my friend Amy Edler. Amy has taken over Edlers Bakery, and she loves strudel!'

Bill replied with a deep bolt of laughter. 'You've taken over Edlers Bakery? Edlers? Now that is a name I have not heard in a very long time.'

Amy followed his lead and gave him a warm smile before replying. 'I'm flattered that you know the name at all, Mr Brooks. It's a pleasure to meet you. Thank you for supporting the children's charity.'

He wrapped his arm around the shoulders of a stunned looking Jared Shaw, and slapped him hard on the back.

'All down to Jared, here—you old dog! Where have you been hiding this little gem? Edlers Bakery! Who would have thought it? Do you know that my father grew up in Vienna?' He beamed a smile at Amy. 'Right around the corner from the original Edler coffee shop! Wait until I tell my mother that I've met up with one of the Edler family! Come and tell me what you're doing in London! Hope you don't mind me stealing your girlfriend for a while, son? Catch up with you later!'

And before Jared could say yay or nay, Bill Brooks had threaded Amy's hand through the crook of his arm and was guiding her through the crowds into a private dining room.

Jared stood in silence as the chatting, smiling strangers filled the space his most important client had left in his wake, and watched as Amy looked over her shoulder with a wry smile, shrugged her shoulders, then turned to laugh at something Bill Brooks said before they were swallowed up by the journalists and photographers enjoying the free food and drink.

The last thing he saw was the slight tilt of her head and a flash of midnight blue silk as she sashayed elegantly away from him. Every movement of every muscle in her body was magnified. Important. As though a searchlight was picking her out in the crowd for him alone.

This was a girl he had only met in person for the first time yesterday, but had heard so much about her from Lucy. This girl had formed a bond with his sister. The kind of connection that could not be broken down by time or distance. He envied her that. One thing was certain. He knew now why Lucy had trusted her friend with something as important as her wedding plans.

Amy Edler was turning out to be one of the most remarkable women he had ever met in his life, and the last ten minutes had only served to increase his admiration.

He was totally in awe.

Then she slipped out of view, leaving him alone, with a glass of warm water in one hand and a party invitation in the other.

And more. His most recent and largest client thought that Amy Edler was his girlfriend.

Strange how he had not rushed to correct him.

Strange that he was even now reliving that moment when her body had been pressed against his arm.

Strange how he was still standing in the same spot five minutes later, watching the space where she had last stood. Waiting. Just in case he could catch a glimpse of her again. The most beautiful woman in the room.

For that he was prepared to wait a very long time.

CHAPTER SIX

'I AM SO sorry to keep you waiting, but Bill is passionate about his business. And…' Amy clutched onto Jared's arm a little tighter '…he has a lot of good things to say about your work.'

'Um. In that case you are both forgiven. Your penance for leaving me at the mercy of Nell Waters is to walk to my car. Do you mind?'

Amy snuggled closer to him. 'Not at all. It's a lovely evening.'

It *was* a lovely evening, and Jared Shaw looked hotter than hot bread.

Her treacherous heart had not yet recovered from that smile when he'd won the auction. But it was enough for her to walk slowly along the pavement, arm in arm with this dazzling man, as he casually chatted to her as though they were old friends and lovers.

'I hear that you're part of Lucy's shopping expedition on Wednesday. It should be quite an event. I'm thinking of alerting the department stores in advance.'

'I'm looking forward to it. We businesswomen don't often get a day off. Work, work, work.'

'Oh, yes, the drudgery of having your hands in sticky flour all day. Thank you for washing them for me.' He tilted his head closer to hers and half whispered, 'you look fabulous, by the way.'

'Thank you, kind sir. My pleasure. You clean up nicely yourself.'

Jared exaggerated adjusting his tie one handed, while dodging the other pedestrians on the busy Covent Garden pavements. 'Oh, this old suit? Found it at the back of my wardrobe. Thought I had better make an effort for the press.'

Amy gave his arm an extra squeeze before quickly changing the subject. 'Did you confirm that replacement wedding photographer?'

'I did. Apparently he owes the other guy several favours. He's happy to do it,' Jared replied, as he negotiated around the pavement café tables. 'Now, may I be so bold as to make a suggestion Miss Edler? Unless you are desperate to get home, I think we should make a small detour. Look across the street. What do you see?'

Amy tore her eyes away from Jared and stared across Covent Garden piazza to the stunning pillars and Greek architecture of a tall stone building.

'The Royal Opera House! How wonderful. Do you know it?'

Jared nodded and looked up into the carved columns.

'Lucy and I used to come here every Christmas as children to see the *Nutcracker*, *Cinderella* or *Swan Lake*. It was magical.'

Amy looked at him in awe. 'Well, you are full of surprises, Mr Shaw. I thought little boys had to be dragged fighting and screaming to watch ballet!'

He nodded. 'Quite right. Except *our* mother knew the background to each ballet—the stories behind the composers and the original performances. Fairy tales. Nursery rhymes. That's what made her such an excellent teacher. We begged her to bring us here. The three of us would dress up in our best clothes and drink cherry lemonade and champagne in the interval. It was better than Christmas Day. Yes, magical.'

There was something is his voice which compelled Amy

to look into his face. There was the young man, so full of hope and dreams.

Then something shifted, a darker memory.

And in that moment the mood changed. His brow was furrowed with anxiety, his mouth moved back to a straight line, and his body almost bristled with tension.

The three of them. Not four. Three. Lucy, Jared and their mother. He had not mentioned his father at all. From the little Lucy had told her, Amy knew their dad had left them when she was ten—which meant Jared must have been about fourteen years old at the time. Her eyes pricked with tears, and she laced her hand with his, forcing apart his fingers, which had tightened into a ball.

Her touch acted like a catalyst, and he ripped his eyes away from the stonework and focused on her face as his fingers relaxed and squeezed hers back, leaving it to Amy to break the silence.

'Those are wonderful memories. How often do you get to see Lucy and your mother? Apart from work?'

'Mum?' He shrugged a reply. 'She gets over to New York once or twice a year. She's happily remarried now, with her own life in France. We'll catch up next week.'

'And what about Lucy? Do you meet up in the office every day?'

'Not at all. I'm either on the road, or she's working on a project with Mike. They run the office for me most of the time.'

Amy stopped and turned so that she was facing Jared. 'I have an idea. You can tell me to mind my own business, but here goes.'

She took a breath as Jared crossed his arms in quiet resolution.

'This time next week your only sister will be a married woman. Right now she is in France, planning to fly over on Tuesday evening. If you were to drive to France and pick her up in person then you would be together for a couple of hours, just the two of you. Sort of a last chance to be together as brother and sister before she starts her new life as Mrs Mike Gerard. Your mum and her family can still arrive on Thursday, as planned.' She gritted her teeth and pretended to duck. 'What do you think?'

Jared unclenched his arms and looked into her face for a few seconds, before replying in a low, intense voice, 'Do you like *La Boheme*? I thought we could go to the opera.'

Amy sighed out loud and grinned, desperate to lift his mood. 'It's my favourite.'

Jared smiled his closed-mouth smile, and then took a firmer grip of her hand as he bit his lower lip. 'Then I'll order tickets for next week.'

'Next week? I thought you were going back to New York?'

'I was,' he replied, looking straight ahead, and clutching her hand even tighter. 'But there's been a change of plan. I might pop over to France and collect Lucy myself, spend some time with her before heading back. So, I'll be here for a few more days—if you can put up with me?'

And with that they walked casually, hand in hand, in silence, across the courtyard, as though it was something they did all of the time.

Jared could never know that her palms were sweating not due to the warm breeze, but to the gentle way in which his fingertips stroked the tender skin on the inside of her palm. Her gaze moved over the happy groups of smiling, chatty couples who strolled across the piazza. Anywhere except Jared. She wanted to look at him so badly it was almost a physical pain.

Except that would mean giving in to the sigh of absolute pleasure which was bursting to escape.

This was what it would be like if she was Jared's girlfriend. On a regular date.

Except, of course, this wasn't a date, was it?

This was a kind gesture to his sister's bridesmaid, who was

going to be standing opposite him in an ancient church next Saturday. That was all it could be. All it was ever going to be.

So, why not enjoy these precious moments and make the best of them while she could? These were the happy memories *she* would hold precious over the coming months, when Jared and Lucy had gone back to their exciting, busy lives and she was merely a person in a wedding photograph.

In a few days she would be back in her normal, safe life. Which was just how she wanted it. Wasn't it?

'Watch out!'

A cyclist swerved towards them to avoid a tourist who had stepped back to take a photograph, and Jared instinctively whipped his body around to block Amy from a blow that never came as the young man wobbled his way around them.

The sudden movement knocked the air out of her lungs, and it was seconds before her brain connected with the fact that she was standing chest to chest with Jared, with both his arms wrapped around her body, her hands flat against his shirt-front.

Just for a moment, Amy closed her eyes and revelled in the warmth and the strength of his embrace. The exquisite aroma of aftershave, antiperspirant and clean pressed linen blended with the musky spice of light perspiration on the warm summer night—and something else. Something unique. Jared. His scent. His heat. And a strange magnetic pull made her want to edge closer and closer to him. A pull that made parting from him so very painful.

The overall effect was totally intoxicating and, light-headed, she felt herself moving forward to rest her brow on his chest. This was her dream, her fantasy. For a few precious seconds she could pretend that she was just like any other girl out for a stroll with her boyfriend. Pretend that this man cared about her, had chosen her, wanted to be with her. Her lover.

That the scars on her chest had never existed.

The scars!

Her heart started racing, the blood pounding in her skull. That cyclist could have knocked her down! Suddenly she was nauseous, faint, and she drew in deep breaths to steady her legs, forcing oxygen to her brain. This was so embarrassing. She would not pass out. Not here, not now. Not with this man.

A strong bicep flexed next to the thin fabric of her dress and her eyes closed in pleasure. It had been so long since she had been held like this!

Drat Jared. She couldn't do this. Why had she agreed to walk with him? He would be flying back to his real world in New York City, and she would back to square one. On her own. Holding it together.

'That was a near miss. Are you okay?' Jared asked, with enough concern in his voice to bring a lump to her throat again.

His hands slid down as she pulled back and smiled up into his face, but instead of stepping away he simply linked his hands behind her back, holding her in place as she recovered.

'A little shaken, that's all. Thank you,' she replied, and made a play of checking his shirt for signs of make-up before hissing, 'You now have blusher on your shirt. Sorry about that.'

Amy leant back so that she could focus, only to find him smiling down at her, his eyes scanning her face from side to side, as though looking for something before speaking. 'No damage done. You still look amazing. Although.'

His lips curved back into a wide smile, so warm, so caring, that she was blinded by it. The fingers of one hand slid up her back as he dropped his head forward and nuzzled his chin against her hair.

Some part of her brain registered that she should make a response, and she forced herself to lift her chin so she was staring at his neck. 'Although?'

His head slid away, far enough so that his eyes could focus

on hers. 'My street cred has just increased by several points. It appears that we have an audience.'

'An audience?' Amy replied, puzzled, and then looked over her shoulder to find a group of older men in dinner jackets, who had been calmly standing outside a brightly lit café, were now giving Jared the thumbs up. She immediately backed away from him, and was rewarded by a round of applause and some manly cheers.

'Your carriage awaits, madam.'

Jared held the door of the British Racing Green luxury sports car, and could not resist holding Amy's hand and enjoying the view as she turned to slide her bottom onto the deep leather seat. Knees together. She had done this before.

The skirt of her dress lifted as she wriggled into position, exposing even more of her long, slim legs, which he simply could not take his eyes off. He was a leg man. Always had been. And these were amazing.

He recovered. 'My company car. Hope you like it.'

'I do—although I should tell you that I do have to be back in the kitchen before midnight, and I wouldn't want this fine machine to turn into a pumpkin.'

'And what about me?' He laughed. 'The frog look is hard to carry off.'

'True.' Amy stroked the leather. 'Very nice. You have excellent taste.'

She waited until Jared had fired up the engine and was out of the underground car park and on the street before speaking again.

'Of course you do realise that your terrible secret is now out in the open?'

Jared swallowed hard. 'Which one? I have so many.'

'No doubt. I was, of course, referring to the vice of choice of you, my driver.' Amy counted out his vices on her fingers. 'Mr Jared Shaw, Company Director.' She waved her fingers around. 'Not averse to a little luxury when it comes to toys for grown-up boys. Does not drink—or at least I've never seen him drink. That cuts out the wine part, which leaves women and song. From what I saw this evening the women part is still going strong, so that only leaves one question. Can you sing?'

He laughed out loud now. A real belly laugh, displaying his perfect teeth. 'Not even in the shower. Never. I was the only boy in my expensive boarding school who had to play in the orchestra in the Christmas musical.'

'Which instrument'?

'The triangle.'

'Seriously?'

He looked at her for a split second, still laughing.

'No. Guitar. A couple of us fancied ourselves as the next boy band. How could we loose? Two tone deaf guitar players. Bound to be a smash hit with the girls at gigs. The fact that we only knew one song was not a factor.'

Now it was Amy's turn to laugh.

'It was incredibly generous of your company to sponsor the event tonight. But one question. Haywood and Shaw Property Management? Okay, I understand the Shaw bit. Who is Haywood? Is he still around? And does he ever come to charity functions?'

'First, I was only too happy to sponsor the event—and second, no, he isn't. And he is an it.'

'Sorry?'

'It's a long story. Why don't I show you instead?'

Jared focused on his driving, turning down one London side street then another, until Amy had lost all sense of direction, before slowing to a halt outside the exact same placard she had seen that afternoon.

They were back at his retail and restaurant development.

Amy was lifted out of her low seat by a pair of strong hands, and she looked around, curious as to why Jared had brought her here at this time of night.

He slipped his dinner jacket around her shoulders and held her within it for a few seconds, bringing up the collar so that he could flip the ultra-soft fabric around her smooth neck.

She pretended not to notice as his fingertips gently moved against her skin to flick the imaginary ends of her hair back over the collar.

'Thank you.' She smiled at him, conscious that the hard cheekbones of Jared's face were highlighted too sharply by the streetlight outside the swish, glossy shopfronts. He was too lean, and she knew that he had eaten almost nothing of the delicious buffet at the hotel.

Maybe she could do something about that if he stayed around long enough?

He smiled too, and surprised her by sliding behind her, so that his arms were wrapped around her waist, holding her tight against him. She felt the pressure of his head against the side of her face as he dropped his chin onto her shoulder, lifted his left arm and pointed.

There was a street sign on the edge of the brick row of terraced houses a little further down the street. She strained to read the letters out loud in the faint light.

Haywood Street.

Amy burst out laughing in surprise, and was about to turn back to Jared when his hand moved to the darkened covered windows of the second floor of the new building.

She sensed the tension in the air, and waited until he was ready to tell her about it.

'Eighteen years ago there was a grotty garage here, with a tiny flat above it. I know that because we lived here. For eighteen months and six days. Lucy, Mum and me. It was the only place we could afford. Frank rented the lower half during the day, and we lived above the garage. The landlord was a complete… Well, he's long gone—but let's just say that the place would have been condemned if it was on the market these days.'

'It must have been tiny.'

'It was! There was only one bedroom, so I slept in the living room. Mum and Lucy shared a single bed. We did the best we could, but we all hated it. I still hate it now. Couldn't wait to leave. So, Haywood Road became Haywood. My sleeping partner.'

Jared whispered the last words, and there was something in the stiffness of his arms around her waist that brought Amy's brows together.

She turned slowly inside the jacket, so that Jared kept his arms wrapped around her waist, and moved forward so that both of her palms were flat on the chest of his dress shirt.

'You named your company Haywood so that you could never allow yourself to forget it. Am I right? You can tell me to mind my own business if…'

He silenced her by lowering his forehead to make contact with hers, giving her time to feel the heat and pressure of his skin and his breath on her face.

A car passed them by, and then a cyclist, on this small road on the outskirts of the city where traffic was part of life. But Amy could hear nothing except Jared's fast breathing as he moved his face from side to side against hers, the stubble on his chin rasping against her cheek for a second before he released his grip on her waist and slowly, slowly, slid his hand up inside the jacket and onto the bare skin of her back above her dress.

The sensation was so unexpected, so delicious, that she inhaled sharply, gasping in air.

It was as though she had given him a signal of approval.

As his fingertips stroked her skin, his soft, sensuous mouth slid slowly and tenderly against her upper lip in the sweetest, most gentle of kisses—so brief that Amy had only seconds to close her eyes and enjoy it before he pulled away from her, moving towards the passenger door of the car, his hand pressed against the small of her back.

'Let's get you home.'

* * *

'So, what time shall we pick you up, baker girl? The dressmaker needs us there around eleven,' Lucy chirped down the phone.

Amy grinned as best as she could, with the telephone jammed tight into the space between her chin and her ear, and her shoulder crushing it in place.

'Can you make it around half-ten? I've got tons to do even though I'm an early riser these days. Like my bread!'

'Oh, very funny. I can't wait to see you in that bridesmaid dress! And then prepare yourself for some serious shopping.'

'Absolutely! Now, tell me about the drive. Did you put up with Jared all the way? Or jump out in Paris and catch a train?'

Laughter on the other end of the phone made Amy smile.

'My brother was charming and brilliant—as usual—and we actually had a great time. Apparently I have you to thank for that! Thanks, Amy. It was special. We hardly argued at all.'

'Aha! Caught you out. So it was not *all* sweetness and light?'

'Oh, we may have agreed to differ on a few things, but nothing we can't fix. I even persuaded him to loan me his apartment for a girly sleep over on Friday night. He'll be moving to the hotel with the boys. Although that has reminded me of something. The flowers for my bouquet. Forget the orchids—that was such a silly idea.'

Amy inhaled sharply, waiting for the big decision. 'And what have you gone for?'

'Roses and lilies. Pale yellow roses. I've just spent two weeks tending my mum's rose garden and I can't get enough of them... Unless, of course, you have already made the sugar orchids. Because I would feel terrible if you had to do it all over again.'

'Not at all,' Amy lied, glancing towards the refrigerator. It held three rather pathetic attempts at yellow and orange sugar orchids, the making of which had occupied most of her previous evening. 'Any chance I could have a sample? That way I can be sure to match the exact shade you need.'

'No problem. I've already asked the florist to send you over the bouquet she suggested—it is absolutely gorgeous! That Elspeth is a genius! Now, I have to dash, Frank is waiting outside with Bella. See you later! And you had better be ready to enjoy yourself!'

Amy managed to negotiate the handset back to its stand without dropping it into the egg whites. She *was* looking forward to talking to Lucy again in person, instead of through telephone calls and e-mails. It had been months since her friend had had a short-notice business trip to London and popped into the bakery to surprise her.

Lucy Shaw, high-flying businesswoman. Lynchpin of Haywood and Shaw, New York.

At one time they had looked like twins. Sleek. Glossy. With the clothing and grooming to match. And tomorrow they were going to the dressmaker for their final fitting before the wedding. How had that happened?

She looked up in time to see a handsome young couple in business suits laughing together as they walked hand in hand down the street, an Edlers carrier bag swinging from the girl's arm like an expensive handbag.

From the side the girl looked so much like the old version of herself that Amy's hand froze on the balloon whisk.

There was a time not so long ago when she had been that girl.

Hard-working, yes, but carefree—happy to go home to an evening of mooching around with the person she cared about, or eating out in bistros and restaurants several times a week.

When was the last time she'd eaten a meal cooked by someone else?

Strange how she had taken it so much for granted at the time. Thought that it would never end. How wrong she had been!

When the phone began to ring, she hesitated before picking it up. There was so much she had to do, and for once it might be nice to sit outside in the sunshine for a few minutes with her coffee.

Drat Jared Shaw for showing her something of what she had been missing.

On the other hand she could hardly afford to miss an order...

'Edlers Bakery.'

'Hello, Edlers Bakery.'

Her foolish girly heart skipped a beat, and her stomach flipped so hard she had to lunge forward to grab the bowl before it slithered off the table.

It was him!

Most of Sunday, Monday and Tuesday had been spent close to the phone. Just in case. And now here he was. The man who had become a permanent player in her dreams for the last four nights.

Breathe. All she had to do was breathe normally. Casual. That was the key. Nice and casual.

'Good morning, Mr Shaw. And what does the weather look like from way up there in that penthouse of yours?'

'I wouldn't know, Miss Edler. Down here on the pavement it's warm, sunny, and actually very pleasant. What are you doing?'

She sucked in a breath. Well, of course he would not waste time calling her from his luxury apartment. Not when Lucy was back in town. He had far more important things to worry about.

'Beating egg whites. One of my chef pals has called in sick. Which is why I now have to create three lemon meringue pies before ten this morning, or his bistro lunch service is toast.'

'Ouch. Edler toast?'

'Of course! And what are *you* doing at this moment?

Planning your next corporate merger? Or designing yet another restaurant conversion?'

There was a chuckle on the other end of the phone.

'Now you come to mention it… No. In fact, I was hoping you would join me, Lucy and Bella for a special lunch today before you hit the shops. My treat. Interested?'

She was so taken aback that she almost dropped the mixing bowl before glancing at her kitchen clock. She had an hour at most to complete her work. Half an hour to shower and change… Maybe she *could* find time to force down food cooked by someone else.

'Tell me more.'

'Ah. A lady who likes to hear the facts before she makes a decision. Good thinking. I seem to remember that you were a big hit with Bill Brooks of Noodles and Strudels the other evening. Well…I have a VIP invitation to the opening of their very first British bistro this very afternoon. Now, how could I possibly think of attending such a prestigious event without the local authority on the subject on my arm? What do you say? Willing to risk being seen out in public with me?'

'Noodles and Strudels are opening today? Wow. Well, how can I resist such temptation? Should be fun!'

'I knew I would find your weakness. Frank will meet you at the dressmakers—and, Amy?'

'Yes?' she replied, drawing the syllable out as long as possible.

'Bill Brooks somehow got the impression that you were my girlfriend. It seems a shame to destroy his illusions. Don't you agree?'

'I live to please. Oh, wait a minute—are you telling me that Bill Brooks will be there in person? Jared?'

He had rung off.

She collapsed down on the edge of the table, oblivious to the egg white dripping onto her trousers, and stared at the handset.

How did Jared do it?

And why did she suddenly feel like bursting into spontaneous laugher?

CHAPTER SEVEN

'WELL, the way Jared tells it, you left my poor brother standing there for a good forty minutes while you were hob-nobbing with the rich and famous! Shame on you, Amy Edler.'

Lucy turned her head to look at Amy over one shoulder as the dressmaker unzipped her from her perfect taffeta silk wedding gown. 'He's not used to being dumped by his lady-friends, you know. It upsets his ego.'

'Lady-friends? Not sure I qualify under that category—and I did apologise for keeping him waiting. Even if I did enjoy myself. I love talking about old Vienna.'

'I'll forgive you—if and only if you agree to catch up over lunch today.' Lucy tilted her head to one side. 'Who knows? Bill might decide to use you as a supplier!'

Amy laughed, but Lucy gestured towards the curtain. 'Okay; now it's your turn to get changed. You have thirty minutes and then we are out of here!'

Thirty minutes was more than long enough as far as Amy was concerned. There had been a time when she'd loved to shop for clothes, and had spent hours trying on outfits. Now? Now she could just about manage it if there was a separate changing room with a solid door and a lock she could control. And even then she did not risk taking off her top.

Not that she had bought many new clothes recently. Why

would she need to? Catering T-shirts and trousers came in packs of ten.

One less thing to worry about.

And one less reason to look at her body.

Amy stared into the full-length mirror and managed a smile. The dressmaker had followed Lucy's instructions to the letter, and the ankle-length oyster silk sheath dress was beautifully cut to accentuate her tiny waist and slim arms, with a small neat neckline and chiffon overlay.

She bent down from the waist and peered into the glass, to check whether her collarbone could be seen from the front. Nothing. Excellent.

Now she could breathe, and relax on Lucy's big day.

And maybe even *enjoy* the wedding.

At that moment she glanced back into the mirror and saw a smiling version of herself in a lovely dress staring back. That version looked happy. Content.

Jared Shaw had a lot to answer for! Maybe that was why she was grinning? One small kiss and she was back in school-girl crush land! How had *that* happened?

Her finger moved over her mouth and traced the point where he had kissed her. Closing her eyes, she could relive the warmth of his body against hers, and the tenderness of his touch—memories which had disturbed her sleep for the past few nights. Just when she needed all the rest she could find!

Noisy chatter outside the cubicle broke into her lovely dream, and she grinned at herself in the mirror as she slithered out of the dress. She was reaching for her skirt when her mobile phone sounded in her handbag.

The last voice she had expected to hear at that moment yelled out at her against a crackling background noise of traffic and people.

'Hello, gorgeous! How are you doing?'

'Ethan? Where are you?'

'Touched down in New York after non-stop from Sydney half an hour ago. Mike had been bugging me about leaving plenty of time before the wedding, and you know what he's like. No last-minute jet lag allowed when it's party time. Especially when you are the best man!'

'Absolutely. That's a long flight,' she replied, desperately trying to regain her composure at the sound of his voice. 'Well, you'll never guess where I am. Trying on my bridesmaid dress. Bella and Lucy are in the next room, with some amazing concoction of a dress. I am sworn to secrecy, but it's a knockout.'

'Didn't expect anything less.' There was a pause. 'Hey, did Lucy mention that I would be bringing my girlfriend to her wedding?'

'Come to think of it, she did mention something about "Ethan and guest". No clue about the details. The least you could have done was fax in a full photo and biography.'

He chuckled, and Amy's heart clenched at the sound as her imagination filled in a picture of the handsome man with sparkling brown eyes and dark, dark hair who had stolen her heart once. He still had some of it. And always would have.

'No need. Ally is flying in tomorrow. I thought I'd give you the heads-up before the wedding. I've finally persuaded the wonderful girl to say yes. You are talking to an officially engaged man! How about that for a shocker?'

Amy sucked air into her frozen lungs before daring to speak in a crackling voice. 'That is wonderful news. Congratulations to both of you. I'm so happy for you.'

'You're the first to know. Wait until we get talking about kite surfing. She's a star! Anyway, limo's here. Have to go. Can't wait to tell you the full story! See you soon!'

'Yes,' she whispered to the silent mouthpiece.

Amy's legs didn't want to support her any more, and she half sat, half staggered onto the padded chair in the changing room, only vaguely aware that she was still in her underwear, clutching the cellphone.

Ethan was engaged. To a kite surfer.

She'd known it had to happen one day. He was bound to find a girl who could love him as much as she had—a girl he could love in return. A girl who shared his passion for water sports. Pity his timing was so bad. Her friend Lucy was getting married in a few days. And now her ex-boyfriend Ethan was headed the same way.

How could things get any worse?

She heard a man's voice outside the changing room, and groaned out loud as the bottom fell out of her stomach and her heart started pounding.

Jared. Of course. He had arrived to escort them to lunch. How was she going to survive eating in the same room as this man when her body was reacting like this?

In frustration and despair Amy shoved her arms into the sleeves of her high-necked silk ruffle blouse, and was buttoning up when Bella's disembodied head appeared through the curtains. Mike's sister had never scored high in the discretion or shyness stakes.

'Jared has turned up to take us all for fizz and food. Almost ready?'

'Be out in a second!'

Bella nodded towards Amy's lower half before pulling back her head. 'Gorgeous knickers, by the way!'

'Who has gorgeous knickers?'

It was Jared's voice.

She was going to kill Bella—unless someone else did it first. The girl might be five years younger than Mike, and about to become Lucy's new sister-in-law, but when was she going to learn some tact? *And* she was supposed to be a journalist.

'Amy. And you shouldn't be listening, you pest.'

'What? I can imagine, can't I? Especially surrounded by all this girly stuff.'

Amy stepped out of the changing room and watched in

silence as Jared picked up a pink monstrosity of a 'ribbon and not much else' corset and waved its hanger vaguely in Bella's direction.

'Good morning, Miss Edler. Ready for a bit of lunch?'

He was wearing a pale blue shirt with the top two buttons undone at the neck, and a dark blue tweed fitted jacket that swished so softly over his arms when he moved that she knew that it had to be cashmere. Begging to be stroked and cuddled into.

Nothing to do with the man inside it.

Not in the least.

Especially not when he waggled the corset in front of Bella and gave her one of those killer grins she had seen him use so effectively at the charity auction. Grins designed to make any girl go weak at the knees and turn to putty in his hands.

Pity they were so effective that Amy was temporarily rendered speechless.

'I hope these dresses are all going to be strapless,' Jared said.

'Not a chance, mate. You'll have to get your dose of boobage somewhere else. We can't wear strapless frocks because of Amy's thing.' Bella waved one hand towards her own generous bosom, and waggled her fingers, before lifting the corset from Jared's hand and wafted it in front of her.

'Amy's thing?' He turned towards Amy and tilted his head to one side, clearly expecting a joke. 'Do tell me more about Amy's thing!'

'Bella!' Lucy had come into the room behind Bella, who turned bright red and rushed out in silence.

'It's okay, Lucy.' Amy turned towards Jared and gave him a small smile. 'I had surgery a couple of years ago and it left me with some scars on my chest.' She shrugged, but her voice was softer, more hesitant. 'I'm a little self-conscious about it, so Lucy agreed to save my dignity with a dress not cut down to South America. That's all. No great mystery.'

Only she glanced down at the floor for just one second longer than necessary before smiling up at him, trying with all that was in her to block out the pain and regret. He was looking at her now with *that* look of pity she knew so well, and suddenly it was all too much.

'Lucy—the dress fits perfectly. Thank you for the lunch invitation, but I do need to get some rest. Call me later.'

And before a frozen Jared or a very startled Lucy could reply, Amy gave her friend a peck on the cheek, snatched her handbag higher onto her shoulder, and walked as fast as she could in her heels—out of the nightmare and into the first taxi she could find.

It was quiet in the empty bedroom. A gentle breeze fluttered the edge of the heavy curtains, bringing with it the welcome sound of chatter and traffic from the street below. The sound of normal people living normal Wednesday afternoon lives.

Amy sat on the floor in the corner of her spare room and stared into pale blue liquid as seahorses and colourful tropical fish swam round and round in the heat from the tiny light-bulb at its base.

Calming, tranquil and serene.

Maria Edler had wanted to throw the nightlight away, or donate the toy to the children's home, when she sold the house and moved to Austria. Amy had insisted that she keep it.

This had been her own nightlight—her constant companion over the years since her lovely mother had given it to her. Perhaps one day another little girl would use it, and find comfort in it as she had?

Her head dropped back against the wallpaper and Amy closed her eyes and tried to calm her body as exhaustion hit hard.

The taxi from the dressmaker had carried her back to a leaking air-conditioner, a fractious and overheated Trixi, and three extra orders. So she'd had to drop everything to complete them in a hurry.

The frantic activity had helped to block out the pain for a while, just as it always did, but that had not lasted long. Not today. The tension in her neck simply refused to go away, no matter how many times she clenched her stiff shoulders up to her ears and then released them. It was not helped by the slippery slide of the silk of her dressing gown against the wallpaper

Amy let the fine silk and lace slide between her fingertips. Ethan had loved to watch her dressing in expensive lingerie, and she had loved to wear it. Loved to feel the silk against her skin, knowing that the man sitting next to her at the breakfast table, with a boyish grin on his face, would hold that image in his head for the rest of the day throughout interminable business meetings.

They had both worked so hard. It had seemed that the only time they could spend together was on holiday at some sunny beach, where Ethan could surf and play volleyball. It was no surprise that Ethan had moved back home to take over the Sydney office six weeks after they'd separated.

At least they had been able to part with a kiss and a warm embrace, and a promise never to lose their friendship. No other woman, no acrimonious insults—just a simple recognition that they had become different people and that it was time for them to move on after four great years together. For that she should be grateful.

Only now he was coming to the wedding with his fiancée. And she had no clue as to how she was going to react to seeing him again.

She slid a little further down the wall.

Why did any of that matter any more?

Who else was going to see the lovely lingerie except her? It was obvious that no lover would stay around long enough to pay attention to her underwear.

Not when they saw what came with the package.

In the meantime she would have to wear these lovely things for herself. That was all.

She could do that. She could paint the ceiling in her spare bedroom wearing burgundy silk underwear.

She sniffed, and then mentally scolded herself.

This was *pathetic*! She was still Amy Frances Cooper Edler. She was still the girl with the first-class degree and the amazing career plan. The same Amy Edler who had flown so high in a perfect sky.

Before a terrified seventeen-year-old gang member robbing a grocery shop had shot her down to earth.

A shaft of afternoon sunlight broke through the curtains and pierced the air. And the raised ribs of the white scar down the front of her chest shone back at her.

A shudder ran down her back, as though a chill wind had smacked into her body, and Amy frantically pushed herself up and stepped into navy blue overalls, throwing her arms into the long sleeves before fumbling with the buttons to wrap it tighter, tighter, tighter around her body, blocking out what she could not face.

She couldn't breathe—couldn't think with her head spinning like this. The last plastic surgeon had warned her about this. Only natural. Bound to happen.

It *wasn't* natural.

She was twenty-eight years old and she couldn't look at her own body without thinking about what had happened that night. The terror, the pain, the look of absolute horror on the face of the boy who had shot her before she passed out.

Seconds. It had only taken a few seconds. And so many people's lives had changed. Tears streamed down her face as she pressed both palms flat against the bedroom wall to support her weight. Gulping down air into her frozen lungs, she felt the tension ease out of her chest.

It would be the second anniversary of the shooting on Friday, and she had coped. Until now.

Lucy was gorgeous, and she had set her heart on a strapless wedding dress. Of course Mike and Lucy knew what she had been through, and she had been thrilled when they'd asked her to be one of the bridesmaids. Lucy had known what she wanted from day one, and what Lucy wanted, Lucy got. Her brother Jared made sure of that. Or at least that was what she had thought.

A few hours ago she had found the truth. The dressmaker had obviously changed the design of the two bridesmaid dresses. Because of her. And on Saturday morning she would be expected to turn up at the family wedding like the bright and sparkling party girl she'd once been.

What a sham. Just like the rest of her life.

No. Not going to happen.

She was overtired. That was it. *Idiot*. The doctors had warned her about overdoing it, and here she was, stressed out because of one simple wedding. And the bride's brother.

Yes. He might have something to do with it.

And now he knew.

Her eyes glazed over, but she could still see the outlines of the bright tropical fish. Had it only been a few days since Jared had walked into her kitchen? It felt so much longer. And soon he would fade and go out of her life. Back to New York and private jets. Back to the life she'd used to have.

Next week things would be back to normal.

In the meantime she had work to do.

Amy wiped away a tear and slammed back the heavy floor length curtains, dragging the heavy fabric along the pole as she unclipped it, so that the June sunlight flooded into the small square room.

This was the same room she had slept in as a teenager in foster care. The room that had become her sanctuary when she'd needed one so badly.

There were so many memories here. The tears, the laughter. Her fingers stroked the familiar patterned wallpaper, with its faded sprigs of pink flowers. This was the very same wallpaper she had come to know and love all of those years ago.

Only that was in the past now. This was not her room any more—this room was for the daughter she had not met yet.

And now it was time to put those sad times behind her. She took a deep breath, flipped open the paint tray, pulled on a glove, loaded her roller, and in one motion completely obliterated the flowers in a solid streak of lavender-white.

Standing back, shocked that she could have committed such a sacrilegious act but not daring to stop, she reloaded the roller and moved quickly along the wall, stretching and bending to cover the complete surface, corner to corner, edge to edge with fresh, clean paint. Sunlight gleamed from the moist surface, filling the room with bright warm light.

A bubble of delight burst through her as she stood back for a moment. Better. Much better. It was going to need several coats, but it was already truly a different room. Only now the ceiling looked dirty. There was one way to change that—and how about some music? But not Elgar. Not today…

In an instant she had found her personal stereo and tuned it to the local radio station.

Grabbing a dining room chair and a paintbrush, Amy hummed along to the pop music blasting out through her headphones, jumped onto the chair, and stretched up on tiptoe to reach the fiddly piece of ceiling around the light. If only she was another six inches taller this would be so much easier!

She gingerly pressed one foot on the arm of the chair, and balanced herself carefully before pointing her brush into the plaster. Excellent. She could not live with a blotchy paint job! Especially when the light fitting was directly over where the bed was going to be! The poor girl would be lying in bed wondering if it was meant to look like that!

Better! She was just about to step down from the rickety dining room chair, when something touched the bare section of skin on her leg.

As she whipped around in shock her left hand grabbed the chair, which wobbled alarmingly at the sudden movement, throwing her completely off balance. At exactly the same time her right hand swung around with the momentum of the movement—and made contact with Jared Shaw's head as he leapt forward to grab her around the middle and take the weight of her body against his.

In the longest few seconds of her life she stared down into his startled face and started to slide down the front of his body, her silk underwear slithering inside her overalls.

He reacted by hunching her up higher, as though she weighed nothing at all, his arms firmly under her bottom as he looked up at what she had been doing.

'Is this what you call resting?'

Amy tried to pretend that it was perfectly normal to have a conversation while being pressed against the pristine shirt of the most handsome and desirable man she had ever met.

'Absolutely. Would you mind holding me up here a little longer? I have a whole ceiling to do?'

He bit his lower lip, as though suppressing a smile, then gently, slowly, slowly, allowed her to slide down the length of his body until her feet touched the floor. His eyes never blinked or left hers, and her breathing seemed to match his. It was a few seconds before he broke the silence.

'Did I ever mention that my first job in the trade was apprentice painter and decorator? And we never, ever stood on chairs. So, you can either buy a stepladder or pass me that roller and let me finish the job. What's it to be?'

Ten minutes later Amy stood next to Jared, hands on hips, and smiled up at the pristine white ceiling.

'Well, I must say you did a reasonable job! Not bad at all,

Mr Shaw. If you ever need a change of direction, I shall be sure to recommend you to all of my friends.'

He gave her a half-bow. 'Why, thank you, madam. I'll keep that in mind. Only if I'm not available, would you please buy a stepladder? Please? For Lucy's sake? She wouldn't want anything to happen to her chief bridesmaid before the wedding!'

'Um. Since you put it like that, I'll think about it. In the meantime…' She glanced over his hair and clothing. 'There is not a spot of paint on you. How do you do that?' She tugged at the sleeve of her overalls, which was already streaked with lavender-white, before muttering to herself, 'Tricks of the trade, I suppose. Did you have a nice lunch with the girls at Noodles and Strudels?'

Jared did not reply, and she looked up at the bewildered man in front of her, who seemed to be staring at her front.

Amy looked down and gasped in horror. The top three poppers on her overalls had come undone, probably during the body slide, revealing the top of her silk camisole and the very top edge of her scar.

She turned her back on him, scrabbling to close the poppers, and then padded into the kitchen to turn the kettle on, not looking back as she lifted tea things from the shelf. Only her trembling fingers let her down and a teaspoon fell to the floor.

Before Amy could reach down to scoop it up she sensed his presence. A strong hand slid each side of her waist, holding her firm. Secure. She breathed in his aftershave and did not resist as he moved closer behind her, until she could feel the length of his body from chest to groin pressed against her back.

His arms wrapped tighter around her waist, the fingers pressing oh-so-gently into her ribcage, and Amy closed her eyes, her pulse racing. It had been a long time. And he smelt fabulous. Felt fabulous.

Jared pressed his head into the side of her neck, his light stubble grazing against her skin, and her head dropped back slightly, so that it was resting on his.

Bad head.

Bad heart.

Bad need for contact with his man.

Bad full-stop.

One of his hands slid up the side of her overall and smoothed her hair away from her face, so that he could press his lips against the back of her neck.

'Lucy was worried about you when you ran out like that,' he said, and his low soft voice sounded different. Strained. Hesitant. 'There were tears from Bella. I didn't know about the scar. I'm so sorry.'

Amy sighed and looked out at the blue sky on the other side of the kitchen window, but sensed her shoulders lift with tension.

'There's nothing for you to be sorry about. It happened and I'm learning to live with the consequences. Besides, I *am* tired. It has been one of those weeks—and serious shopping would be hard work, you know!' The joky tone of her voice sounded flat. False.

Jared continued to breathe into her neck, and one of his hands slid up from her waist to move in small circles on her shoulder. The room began to heat up at a remarkably rapid rate.

'I know you're tired. So does Lucy. She sent me here to check up on you, with a note for the lovely Trixi. Although I still had to use the full force of my charm to persuade her to open the door and let me in. I don't think she trusts me.'

That did make Amy grin. 'Trixi the virtue-keeper. I like that.'

Jared said nothing, but the hand running in circles slid down her arm from shoulder to wrist and he moved impossibly closer, his hand moving slowly up and down her arm.

'This is a seriously unattractive garment. With one hell of a woman inside it. I'm seeing a new side of the baking business. Please tell me you don't wear gorgeous knickers under those hideous navy T-shirts!'

Amy smiled wide enough for Jared to sense her movement. 'Of course not. This is off-duty lingerie. Speaking of which…'

She slowly lifted one of Jared's hands from her waist and pushed gently away from him, instantly sorry that she had broken the touch. She turned back to face him.

Without her shoes, her head came up to his chest, and she stepped back so that she could look into the smiling, quizzical, handsome face. Of a truly nice man.

'I do need to finish the painting. I'm sorry if I upset Lucy. I'll call her.'

Jared decided to do something useful with his arms, crossing them in front of his chest while staring down the back of her gaping overalls. In silence.

She couldn't help it. She clutched the two fronts of her overalls tight together, and glared at the man who was clearly oblivious.

She bent down so her head was at the same level her chest had been. 'I'm up here. And *this* is the reason I like privacy when I decorate!'

He had the good grace to look guilty.

'Busted.' He smiled, and then dodged when she tried to thump him in the chest—only to find he had half turned playfully at the last minute, so that her fists collided with a very solid shoulder.

The smile on his lips faded and his tongue flicked out to moisten his upper lip. Amy knew that move. He couldn't be nervous. *Could he*?

Amy poured boiling water into the cafetière of fresh-ground coffee before saying in a low voice, 'What is it, Jared? What are you really doing here?'

CHAPTER EIGHT

His eyebrows lifted. 'Am I that obvious?'

She nodded and took another cup from the shelf, waiting for his answer.

'Out with it,' Amy said, keen to hear the true reason for his visit. 'What's your plan?'

'Okay. Well, first I wanted to thank you for your suggestion that I drive Lucy over from France. We haven't made that kind of connection in years.'

'And?'

'It was great. We both know that things are going to change, but I'm happy for her.'

'Did you fight?'

He broke into a wide grin and pressed one hand over his heart as though wounded. 'Me?' Then he chuckled. 'Twice. And both times it was about the same thing. Our father. Eric.' The chuckle faded and he looked hard into Amy's face. 'Which is why I need you to back me up with Lucy on Friday night. At the family dinner.'

Her hand paused over the coffee and she turned to him. 'The wedding dinner? But your whole family will be together for once. And I'm only the bridesmaid!'

'Hardly that. But you're right. It has been years. And that's part of the problem.' Jared glanced down and found something fascinating to pick off the sleeve of his shirt. 'You've known my sister since university. What did she tell you about our father? Our early life?'

Amy shrugged. 'I know that your father was some sort of accountant. Her story is that he was arrested and sent to prison for embezzlement, but she has no memory of that. Your mum divorced him, and started a new life. In fact…' she paused for a second as the realisation hit her '…she was only ten when he left. You and your mum have been the only family she has known for most of her life.'

'You're right. Lucy *was* only ten when we traded down from a five-bedroom mansion to the one-bed flat above a garage I talked about the other night. I had to leave my private boarding school. Lost most of my friends, teachers—everything I had come to know. And something else—more important. I thought my dad was the best man on the planet. I was wrong. It turned out that he was a crook. A con-man. Through and through.'

Jared shook his head, smiled, and focused on the coffee. 'And he wasn't even a very clever crook, so I'd lost out to the local lads on that score as well. You aren't supposed to get caught.'

He lifted his head and looked into her eyes. 'Lucy has no idea of the kind of man he was. Mum wanted her to keep some fanciful illusion that her dad had made some bad decisions and was serving time for that. That he wasn't the evil, greedy man the press and the trial judge said he was. Just someone who had made mistakes.'

He sniffed and looked around the room. 'He was a drunk, Amy. Who liked to gamble with money he didn't have. It took me a long time to realise that fact.'

'That must have been so hard. I had no idea.'

'No reason for you to. Lucy wasn't old enough to see it for herself.'

She sat back in her chair and waited a few seconds before replying. 'Why are you telling me this, Jared? Why now?'

He tilted his head towards her. 'My father was released

from prison on parole a few years ago. Mum and I agreed that we shouldn't tell Lucy. Her kind heart and good intentions could have caused a lot of problems. As far as she knew he was still in prison. Until today.'

He slowly raised one hand and slid it up and down the side of his cup. 'It seems that the old man has been living in South Africa, reading the English newspapers. He saw the announcement about the wedding and decided that he had the right to see his only daughter getting married. As though he can decide to turn up and get a hero's welcome. Well, he lost that right a long time ago.'

Insensitive to the hot coffee, Jared was clutching the porcelain cup so tightly Amy was afraid it would be crushed between his powerful hands.

She pressed her own hands around his, forcing him to look at her. And what she saw in those eyes made the breath catch in her throat.

The pain of the boy who had lost his precious father, his life, his future. It was all there for a fraction of a second, before the walls came up again and the smile lines creased around his eyes.

'So is your father coming to London?'

'He's already here. Lucy took a call from him right after lunch. She was excited—can you believe that? She was actually thrilled that he wanted to be here for her big day. So thrilled, in fact, that she invited him to the dinner on Friday. I want to be there for her, but I don't know if I can shake that man's hand. And it will break her heart if I don't.'

The room around them appeared to expand, to hold in the suppressed energy and despair in those eyes, and Amy swallowed down her own fear before speaking.

'How can I help?' she whispered. 'What do you want me to do?'

He looked into her eyes and gave her a real smile. From the heart.

'Come to the family dinner on Friday night. As my date.'

'Your *date*? You want your family to think that I'm your girlfriend?' Amy looked across the table in astonishment. 'What about your date for the wedding? Won't she be a tad upset?'

The smile on his face faltered. 'I don't have a date for the wedding. You must have a very poor opinion of me if you thought I was paying you attention when I had someone back in the States. How did that happen?' He paused. 'Did Lucy tell you that I was seeing someone? Is that it?'

Amy shook her head. 'No, no—she didn't. I'm sorry. The guest list says "Jared Shaw and guest", and that hadn't changed as of this morning.'

Jared sighed loudly, pulling a slim palmtop computer out of his pocket and turning it around so she could see the display. 'I spend eight months of the year travelling to building sites wherever Haywood and Shaw are responsible for a project, and the other four months working twelve-hour days to generate more work. That doesn't leave a lot of time for socialising outside work, and even if it did…most of the women I meet are either married, engaged or putting in the same hours as I am to build their own career. This is my diary for the rest of the year. Feel free to take a look at it. Please.'

Shuffling closer in her baggy overalls, Amy managed to peer at the numbers, dates and locations displayed in tables on the screen before exhaling slowly.

'Four sites across the American mid-west in the next five months. One week in France in September… Ah—of course. That would be your mother's birthday. Then New York, and back to London in December to work with Bill Brooks on his Phase Two.'

She slid back to her own chair and bit her lower lip, while keeping her eyes firmly fixed on her coffee.

'It wasn't my intention to offend you, Jared, but you are

a wealthy and very attractive man. I'm surprised you don't have a date for the wedding. That's all.'

'Thank you for noticing—and I'm not offended. Besides, you were sent a similar wedding invitation to mine—"Amy Edler and guest". Am I mistaken? Unless you have a secret boyfriend, it seems to me that we are both in the same boat.'

She looked up as he slowly closed down his computer and smiled across at her, before speaking in a low, warm voice.

'You are a stunning and talented woman, Amy, and I'm amazed you are still single. Amazed and delighted. I'm a lucky man. So will you eat dinner with me on Friday evening as my date? Please say yes.'

Incredibly, she stopped herself from jumping onto his lap and kissing him senseless.

Bad brain.

Bad sensible girl.

'Before I answer that question I have to know something. Would I be there as a decoy to distract you from your father? Or as a holding-hands-under-the-table-and-cuddling date? Or both?' Her eyes flicked up and locked onto his. 'Just so I'm clear. I'm sure you'd agree that there is an important difference between the two.'

Crinkles appeared at the corners of his eyes—those deep, dark, twinkling and smily eyes.

'I would be happy to hold your hand under any table you care to specify, Miss Edler. But for this event—yes, it would be both. I need you there.'

He needed her. He needed her.

'Okay, I will be there for you. But only as your friend and as Lucy's bridesmaid—not your girlfriend.'

I want to be; oh, I so want to be.

She pushed herself to her feet, straightened her back. 'And now that is *quite* clear, can I *please* finish my painting? I need to get the room finished for the end of next week, in case my assessment is brought forward.'

Jared froze. 'Assessment? Are you looking to remortgage this place?'

'Oh, no—thank heaven. Something far more important.' Amy broke out into a stunning grin of delight. 'I need to convince Nell Waters that a single girl can give a child a loving home. That's all.'

Jared collapsed back down on his chair as though someone had popped a balloon and released the strings that had been holding him up. 'Foster or adopt?' he replied in a weak voice.

'Adopt, if I can. An older girl would be great, but Nell is looking for the right placement. I can hardly wait. It has taken me two years to get this far in the process. So thank you for helping with the ceiling.'

'Um, you are most welcome, Amy. Right. Yes.' He exaggerated looking at the designer watch on his wrist. 'Must dash. Frank should be delivering Lucy and Bella back to the hotel any minute. Have to get back.'

Her frown deepened as she watched him tug on the cuffs of his shirt in fraught silence. 'Is there anything wrong? Jared?'

Something fascinating in his laptop bag held his gaze. 'Wrong? Why should anything be wrong.'

Amy walked slowly up to this tall, handsome, powerful man, and carefully lifted his hands away, so that she was facing him, chest to chest.

'The other day at the children's home. It wasn't the first time you had been there, was it?'

There was a sharp inhalation of breath before he shook his head.

'Four days. Mum was in hospital with gastric 'flu. Frank was working in the north somewhere and it took him a while to track us down.'

He looked down into her eyes and his fingers clenched around hers. 'They were the worst four days of my life. If you ever want to know the reason I drive myself day and night to make my business a success, that would be a good place to start.'

She tilted her head so that she could look into his face and smiled. 'You have come a long way from Haywood Street and Ashcroft Grove, Jared. Isn't that something to be proud of? You can put the past behind you once and for all.'

He released his hand so that he could lift the fingers up to her cheek in silence.

'You are quite remarkable. Do you know that? You have this business, this workload, and yet you want to sacrifice your time and your life to give a young person a second chance. I admire you for that. But do you truly know what you are getting into?'

'Better than most. The Edlers were a terrific family, and Maria did everything she could to help me. But when she adopted me I was still angry and grieving for the parents I had lost. I know the first twelve months are going to be very hard. It will take time for a child to learn that she can trust me.'

Amy led Jared across to a collection of framed photographs. 'These are my birth parents, on holiday in Cornwall. I'm the freckle-faced toddler in shorts.'

He picked up the photo, glanced at it, then smiled down at Amy as he passed it back to her. 'Cute. Very cute. The potential was there. And your parents look like a happy couple.'

'I think they were.' She nodded to a larger photograph. 'This is the Edler clan at the family Christmas in Vienna last year. There must have been about thirty of us all together, and it was brilliant.' She suddenly laughed out loud. 'Of course I have had to warn Nell that the girl she chooses is bound to be *seriously* spoilt by her adoptive grandparents! *This* is the family I want to bring a child into, Jared. My new family can become *their* new family. Is that so very wrong?'.

Jared studied the photograph for a few seconds before replying. 'No. It's not wrong. Just the opposite. It's probably the best thing you can do. Because one thing is very clear. From what you have just told me there is no room for a man in your life. And that, pretty lady, does not make any sense to me at all.'

His fingers stroked her cheek as he looked deep into her eyes. 'I do have to go, but I'll catch up with you tomorrow. Four o'clock, after you'd been to Clarissa's. And try not to work all evening!'

Then he released her, turned with one backward glance, and closed the door behind him—leaving Amy to simply stare at the space where he had been standing.

The remainder of Wednesday, and Thursday morning, had been a blur of action for Amy. The decorating had been completed, the bakery had been packed with customers and orders, and the phone had never stopped ringing with calls from Lucy, Mike, and a tearful Bella.

It had been a joy to escape the heat and frantic activity of the bakery for a few precious hours, and saunter along the warm streets to see Elspeth, who'd been a lot calmer than the last time—even if she had been a tad surprised to see that Amy wasn't pregnant after all, and thought she must have mistaken her for someone else.

Amy skipped along the street in the warm sunshine, swinging an Edlers carrier bag from one hand. A wolf whistle rang out from behind her in the street, and she gave a small bottom waggle in reply, well aware of the source of the whistle.

As she'd predicted, a familiar man caught up with her and hooked his arm around hers.

'I hope you don't do that to all the boys, pretty lady. Although the view *was* spectacular.'

'Of course I do. How else do I entice customers to my shop? Works a treat. And you can let go of my arm now.'

She glanced over. Jared was wearing a sexy striped blue and white shirt designed to show off his tan. He looked hotter than a loaf straight out of the oven, and her silly girly heart jumped a beat.

'Not a chance. I needed security the last time I walked down this street. Besides—' he made a show of leaning his head into her neck, making her skin bristle with the feel of his stubble '—I need practice before our date tomorrow evening. And may I say that you look spectacular, Miss Edler? Although I still prefer the outfit you were wearing to paint the ceiling. Unless, of course, you are still wearing it…'

He pulled them both to a lurching halt, and his eyes scanned her body as he stood on tiptoe, pretending to peer down her top.

She fluttered her eyelids at him, well aware that she was blushing like crazy. 'Thank you. And I might be—but there is no way you are finding out for yourself, so learn to live with the disappointment.'

He gathered her arm again, and turned his head forward. 'Spoilsport. Of course I *do* have a vivid imagination, and gorgeous knickers always do it for me. GK. Remind me to thank Bella for that image.'

'Yes, very funny. Now, behave yourself. You'll be pleased to hear that everything is still on track for Saturday. Elspeth's done a good job overall, and it was not her fault that our photographer had a better offer to film rare wild camels in Mongolia.'

'No dedication, some people.' He paused and clutched her arm tighter. 'You do look wonderful.'

'Seriously?'

'Seriously. And sorry about yesterday. I had no right to blackmail you with my tales of woe. I will understand if you change your mind about tomorrow.'

She focused on putting one sling-backed linen shoe in front of the other for a few seconds, well aware that neither of them was prepared for eye contact.

'You are forgiven. I know you want Lucy to be happy on her wedding day, and if Lucy truly wants her dad there—well, this is *her* day. She has the right.'

'Um. Not so sure about that. But we have far more important matters to discuss. May I suggest a short stroll on this lovely day?'

And, his fingers meshing with hers, they walked hand in hand, as though it was the sort of thing they did every day of the week.

Amy was too terrified to look at Jared, and forced herself to inhale slowly—despite the sudden urge to scream and jump, and shout to the world that Jared Shaw was holding her hand.

In public.

In daylight.

On the street.

What was more, he had yet to comment on the fact that her pulse was racing and her hand was sweaty.

She was so engrossed in placing one foot in front of the other that she almost missed a step when he started talking to her.

'I bet you missed your lunch today. I went to Giorgio's, which was as good as ever.'

'You went to Giorgio's? *Oh.*'

Just the thought of that wonderful Italian food set her tummy rumbling, and she instinctively pressed one hand to her stomach before she realised that Jared might notice.

Jared noticed. 'Thought so. Too busy working to eat. Not good. You need to keep your strength up. My sister is relying on you for that wedding cake.'

He nodded towards her carrier bag as they stopped at a crossing, and pulled it open at the top to peer inside.

'Anything edible in there?'

She waggled the bag from side to side. 'Two croissants Elspeth couldn't manage. Why do you ask? Feeling peckish?'

'Did you know that my apartment block is the other side of this park? And that Giorgio's does take-away? We can sort out any last-minute glitches on the plan.'

'Giorgio does not do take-away.'

'He does for special customers.' And he grinned at her and squeezed her hand as they moved under the shade of some beech trees.

'Come on. Let's give the ducks a real treat. Edlers croissants. Hand delivered by the baker herself.' He glanced towards her feet. 'Those shoes are as good as the knickers. Do you think your toes will survive another ten minutes in this heat?'

She looked at her grey linen shoes and tried to move her swollen toes, which were more used to wide clogs. She sighed in exasperation, then pointed to Jared's loafers.

'I plan to become one of those charming old eccentric ladies who walk the streets in their carpet slippers because they are comfy and their stiletto-induced bunions are causing them trouble. My pockets will be stuffed with hand-made confectionery, and children will either love me or run off screaming in fear. The ducks will think I am a goddess.'

'I can see it now. You will be gorgeous. Speaking of ducks…'

A pair of mallards was already out of the water and coming their way, followed by a line of fluffy brown and gold ducklings.

'Prepare the croissants!' Jared clutched her closer to him and grabbed her bag. 'We may have to fight our way out.'

An hour later Amy leant on a stunning wrought ironwork balcony and looked out over the trees of a small park to the rooftops and busy streets of the city she loved, with sunlight reflecting from high windows and roof tiles.

The ducks had been fed to bursting, the sun was still shining, and she had taken her shoes off. Bliss.

A light breeze caught a spicy fresh fragrance from the tubs of foliage plants and trailing hot-pink geraniums, their blossoms spilling from varnished hardwood tubs next to spotless patio furniture.

It was a lovely spot, and for a moment Amy felt a pang of jealousy for anyone who had the opportunity to live here and enjoy this terrace every day. It would be magical to eat breakfast on this balcony on a summer morning.

She closed her eyes and revelled in the feel of the sun on her skin.

It had been so long since she had taken time out to sunbathe or relax. Where had summer come from? One minute it was snowing and raining, and the next this. Where had all the months gone? Where had her life gone?

Amy clutched onto the metalwork and wrapped her fingers tightly around the rail.

She had made her choice. She flicked open her eyes, and the first thing she saw was tiny flakes of croissant on her sleeve.

Suddenly she knew that she didn't belong here, in this luxurious penthouse, overlooking some of the most expensive real estate in the world.

She had belonged once. When she'd been Amy the banker. Amy the sophisticate. Amy the girl who'd spent a fair amount of her wages every month on manicures, haircuts and waxing, to create the perfectly groomed exterior expected of a woman dealing with wealthy clients.

The memories of the wasted hours she had spent in salons across America made her smile—until she inspected her short, functional nails.

Not now. Now she wanted to be back within the safe four walls of her bakery. Where she had built her new life.

Damn Jared Shaw for breaking through her comfort zone. For making her notice that there was another life around her. For making her…feel.

'What do you think of the view?' Jared's voice startled her, and she turned away from the view and back to the real world.

'Amazing! How did you manage to wangle the penthouse flat?'

'I was looking for somewhere special.'

'Well, you've certainly got that.'

'Yes, I'm going to miss it. Food will only take a few minutes.'

Amy watched from the kitchen table in the huge open plan space, and tilted her head to one side. 'What do you mean? Going to miss it?'

'This whole flat is one giant showhouse for my last development project in East London.' He shrugged his shoulders. 'That work is over, and this place will be on the market next week. Then I'm out of London for good.'

'Wow. Do you have a home in New York to go back to?'

'Sure. I own a building. Hope you like herb linguine?'

'Thank you, yes—I love it.'

Jared lowered the pasta into boiling water, then sprinkled in a pinch of large white salt crystals before pressing a toggle on a high-tech version of an egg timer.

'Do you like to cook? You seem to know your way around a kitchen.'

'Lucy probably can't remember some of the amazing concoctions I came up with when we were kids. Mum didn't finish work until seven most nights, so I was in charge of what was loosely called dinner.'

'Well, that's one way of learning to cook.'

'Oh, I had books. The local library was brilliant for that. I soon learnt the joys of dried pasta and supermarket special offers. And soup. Got to love soup. It's amazing what you can do with stock cubes and some tins.'

Amy looked over his shoulder to see what he was doing. The pain and sorrow in his voice had touched something very deep inside her. This was the closest she had come to the real Jared Shaw. No pretence. No jokes. Just Jared standing in a kitchen cooking pasta. One thing was for sure. He did not want any woman's pity—so she was not going to give him any.

She deliberately stepped away and started opening kitchen cabinets. 'Why don't I cut the bread and lay the table? As long as you don't mind me rooting around in your kitchen?'

Jared swirled one hand into the air around his head. 'Feel free to root as much as you like.'

'I bet you say that to all the girls.'

'If I did, you would be the first woman to actually take me up on it and do anything close to cooking here. Didn't you know? Eating at home is out of fashion these days. But don't mind me. You'll find cutlery in that drawer.'

Amy gave a mini-curtsey. Which was a mistake.

Because at that precise moment Jared raised his arms to lift two plates from the shelf, and in the process his shirt rose high enough above the waistband of his low rise jeans to reveal a couple of inches of toned flat stomach. The last time she had seen abs like that was at a modelling agency her banking firm had used for some promotional material. They'd been shooting a male stripper calendar in the same studio.

Why was it that she had always been attracted to the athletic type? Jared had spent years in the building trade. Was it any surprise that he kept fit? Just when she thought that he could not be more gorgeous, he had to hit her with this. The irony of it all made her sigh out loud.

'What? Was it something I said? Or have you found a new hobby down there?'

Amy hesitated before replying, desperate to avoid the harsh truth.

'I love my bakery so much it's hard to imagine just giving up my home and moving to another country. I mean, you have cars here—furniture and stuff! What happens to all of that?'

Jared chuckled. 'Have I ever mentioned my admin team? All organised. Please don't worry about it. I'm used to living out of a suitcase.'

For a moment she wanted to run into Jared's arms, feel the strength of his body against hers, and tell him how attracted she was to him. This man who only a few minutes earlier had told that he was leaving London for good.

She couldn't risk going through that rejection and pain again.

To see that pity in Jared's eyes would break her heart. She had to control herself and fight this powerful attraction. She just had to. His life was in the fast lane of the city she had left behind her.

Time to put the mask back on and swallow down her feelings.

Amy watched in silence as Jared stirred the pasta sauce.

'That smells wonderful.'

'Oh, there's more. You'll find some foccacia in that bag. Giorgio claimed he made it himself, but you have shattered all my illusions on that front, so I await your expert opinion.'

Jared watched as Amy lifted out the loaf and brought it up to her face, inhaling deeply.

'Fantastic. Oh, yes, he made this. I don't do foccacia. I mean, I could—but this is good. Did you see the olive oil? His brother makes a first pressing. It's wonderful.'

'Feel free to eat. You must be starving.' Jared checked the sauce, then glanced back over his shoulder just as Amy slowly closed her lips around a piece of the bread and groaned in pleasure, her eyelids flickering as her face twisted in delight.

It was the sexiest thing Jared had ever seen in his life.

Giorgio would be able to retire on the take-away orders coming to this flat—because there was no way Jared was going to sit opposite this woman in a restaurant if she was going to do *that* with her food.

He froze, stunned, and tried in vain to control his breathing—and various other parts of his anatomy which seemed to have woken up to the fact that he was within arm's reach of an amazing woman, and they were alone in his apartment.

His heart was racing hard and fast as he stepped across to the refrigerator and took a breath of cool air, fighting to regain his composure. This was getting out of hand—and all he was doing was *looking* at Amy!

It had been a very long time since he had wanted to be with a woman as much as he did at that moment.

Amy rustled around behind him, finding cutlery and humming gently to herself as he pretended to move the meagre contents of his huge refrigerator around.

Was this what it would be like?

To have someone who loved you and wanted to be with you? Not just for an afternoon between international flights, but seven days a week? He had only met this woman a few days ago and the connection was…what was it? A crush? It was a lot more than physical attraction, that was for sure.

In a few days he would back to his normal life across the Atlantic. This flat would be sold, and his time here would be a memory. Left to his imagination.

If this was what Amy did with foccacia, what would she be like in his bed? Naked, with his hands running over the soft skin of her stunning body, giving her pleasure.

Suddenly Jared found an excellent reason to plunge his head inside the chiller.

'I have white wine if you would like some,' he said, casually waving the sealed bottle that had sat there for the last year, waiting for Lucy to drink it.

'Thank you, but I have tons of work to do tonight. Need to keep a clear head.'

He closed the door and looked at her, slack-jawed. 'You're serious. You are actually going back to *work*?'

'Of course. Now, you have *got* to try this foccacia before the pasta.' And without asking or waiting for a reply she slid off the stool and held a piece of bread in front of his mouth. Fragrant rosemary and salt filled his senses, and without thinking he leant forward and closed his lips around her fingertips.

The silence between them opened up.

Then the timer went off and he swallowed, suddenly desperate to keep Amy close to him as long as he could and eke out the precious time they had left together.

'That *is* good. Ready for some linguine, madam? And then we need to start work on the real business for the afternoon. Where am I going to find personal presents for the bridesmaids and the wedding planner. Any ideas?'

CHAPTER NINE

JARED looked up at Amy, and they both burst out laughing at the thought of buying a gift for Clarissa.

Wiping her eyes, Amy shrugged her shoulders before replying. 'I'm happy to help with the wedding. No present required. After what Lucy and Mike did for me after the accident, it's the least I could do.'

'Why do you say that?'

She paused and lowered her fork. 'What did Lucy tell you about—you know—my accident?'

'Nothing. She never said a word.'

'Two years ago I was working in Chicago, and I had arranged to meet up with some colleagues after work. Only fate had other plans. Fate in the shape of a seventeen-year-old boy called Dan, who had been persuaded to rob a grocery shop as part of his gang initiation ceremony. I walked in. He shot me. I woke up in a hospital bed, with Mike and your sister taking turns to sit by my bedside for the best part of a month.'

Jared slid from his chair and stood behind her, his arms wrapped around her waist and head resting on one shoulder.

'I'm so sorry, Amy. I can't imagine what that was like. Sorry you had to talk about it. I'm sorry I brought it up.'

'I am fine with talking about it, Jared. It happened and there is not one thing I can do to change that. And it was fate. If I hadn't been shot I would never have come back here. Kismet.'

He swallowed down hard, stunned by the calmness of her voice, and pressed his forehead against her short chestnut curls. 'I don't understand. Why didn't Lucy tell me?'

'I asked her not to tell anyone, and she kept her promise. I was a mess, Jared. You know Lucy almost passed out when she saw me for the first time? It was horrendous, but she was there for me. You should be proud of your little sister. She deserves happiness on her wedding day.'

Amy sighed, shook her shoulders, and switched the sunshine smile back on as she turned in his arms.

'So, you see, I owe Lucy. And Mike. And what's more they were really supportive of my idea of being a baker instead of a boring executive. No offence.'

'None taken. Wow. I didn't think Lucy would have the stomach for that. Maybe she is capable of surprising me after all.' His napkin touched her face, where a single tear had escaped, then continued to stroke her cheek. 'How are you now? What do the doctors say?'

'That you are looking at a very lucky girl. Another inch either side—' She made a slicing motion with her hand. 'Full recovery. Apart from the post-traumatic stress of course.' She laughed out loud. Her laughter sounded hollow through the pain in her throat.

Jared reached out for her, but she slid away and stood up to gather the bowls. No pity. Not if she wanted the floodgates to stay closed. 'So, no present needed.'

He seemed to get the message.

'In that case, would you consider a personal gift from the bride's brother?' He paused, and the tone in his voice changed. 'In fact, I may have done something a little rash.'

'Am I going to like this?' Amy asked warily.

'You know our good friend, Frank Richards?'

'Chauffeur to the stars? Yes. Is he still driving Lucy to the wedding?'

'Try and stop him. It's not that.'

He paused. 'Now, don't scream or shout. I simply mentioned to my old mate Frank that there was a lovely lady called Hannah who was in need of some loving care and attention. That was all.'

Amy froze, then turned to him with both hands on her hips. 'He hasn't…?'

Jared raised his hands in the air. 'He would not dream of touching her rusty sides without your permission. No way. He simply said that he would take a look and give us an idea of how long it would take to bring the old girl back to full health.'

'And that's all? Simply take a look?'

Jared nodded.

'He wouldn't tow her off to the crusher?' Amy shivered.

'No chance.'

Her shoulders dropped, and she thumped Jared on the arm. 'Stop scaring me like that! I hate to say it, but that is probably a good idea. I trust Frank. He won't try and rip me off. Yes, okay—he can take a look at Hannah.'

She narrowed her eyes and glared at Jared as she cleared the plates. 'He's already done it, hasn't he?'

'I said it was rash. He's promised to call me tonight with the damage.'

'You? Why not get back to me?'

'Think of it as my personal present. Hannah is going to have a full face-lift, liposuction, tummy tuck. The works. On the house, as it were.'

Amy sat back heavily in her chair. 'Have you any idea of how much that would cost?'

'Yes. I have. You're forgetting I used to work with Frank. If I had the time I would probably do it myself, as a weekend project, but Frank will do a good job for you. No problem.' He leant forward and smiled that certain smile, only inches from Amy's face. 'I can't bear the thought of Hannah sitting outside for another winter, rusting away, getting older and older, until it is too late and—'

'Okay, okay. You've made your point. And I *was* intending to get around it. Most of my customers collect their orders, but the big restaurants insist on deliveries, and I want to build up that part of the business. I suppose I could rent a van while the work is being done.'

Jared shook his head.

'How long is it going to take? Months?'

He reached into his pocket and picked out a set of car keys. 'You can have my SUV for as long as you need it. I don't need it any more, and Frank tells me that the resale value is terrible. What do you say?'

He dangled the keys in front of her, but she pushed her hands under her bottom as she shook her head. Those keys were far too tempting.

'I'll say thank you for the kind offer—but no, thank you. You've been far too generous already. In fact I was going to ask a favour, but you beat me to it with Hannah.'

He tried to keep it casual by dropping the keys into her bag and shrugging.

'The keys are there if you change your mind. And ask me anyway. I can only say no. Coffee?'

'Please.' She paused. 'I don't like asking people for help. Goes against the grain.'

'I noticed. Which makes it even more intriguing. Come on—what could be more important than Hannah? New shopfront? Holiday in the Bahamas? Out with it.'

'You're in property development, right?'

'Right.' His hand slowed over the coffee pot.

'So you know about building work? Refurbishment?'

'That's the bulk of my work. What do you need? An extension? New roof? Yours is not looking too healthy, by the way.'

'Trixi's mother who is disabled. She needs that shower. I thought you might have some contacts who would charge a fair price.'

Jared stopped dead and turned to face Amy. He looked at her in silence, his face calm, serious.

'You are a remarkable woman, Amy Edler.'

He picked a pad and a pen out of a drawer. 'I need her full address and the name of the landlord. There will be a Haywood and Shaw team knocking on her door Monday morning at nine sharp to draw up the plans.'

'Seriously?'

'Consider it done.'

Amy flung her warm arms around Jared's neck and kissed him heartily on the cheek. 'Thank you. Thank you so much. You get the phone. I'll make the coffee.'

She released him so suddenly he almost fell back, and he could only watch as she snatched up the paper and began writing down the address furiously.

He couldn't help wondering what he would get if he offered to provide a new kitchen at the same time?

Amy sauntered into the living room, wiping her hands on a teatowel, intending to ask whether he wanted more coffee on the terrace.

Jared was stretched out on a huge, extra-long sumptuous leather sofa.

Asleep.

His thin leather-soled shoes had been shuffled off onto the fine hand-made rug.

Time stilled as she stood there, silently watching his chest rise and fall, the muscles taut under the stretched shirt fabric. As she gazed at that handsome stubbly face and the seriously seductive full lips something twisted below her waist, and her poor wounded heart skipped several beats.

Jared stirred and turned slightly as she picked up his jacket and without thinking raised the fabric to her face and inhaled. A totally sensual aroma flooded her senses. Leather, spicy aftershave, fresh laundered clothing—and something else.

The same intense smell she had picked up in the air, when he'd lunged closer to her, and again when he had held her body close to him only a few hours ago. She closed her eyes and revelled in the aroma. This was Jared. What would it be like to press her face against the skin of this man fresh from the shower?

Whoa! Her eyes flashed open and she held the jacket as far away from her body as her arms would allow. Stop that! *Idiot*!

Now, get out of here. Right now! Before he wakes up and catches you sniffing his things. How pathetic would that be?

She sighed.

And woke him up.

'Oh, no. How long was I out?' he asked, swinging his legs over the end of the sofa as he raked his fingers through his hair. 'My apologies. What terrible manners.'

'Only a few minutes—and there is nothing to apologise for. You have had a busy few days, and jet lag is finally catching up with you.'

'You are being far too forgiving. It's bad enough that you are doing the work while I am lying here. Come and sit and talk to me about life while I wake up a little.' He patted the sofa cushions and tried to snatch her fingers to draw her down to the comfortable seat, but she dodged back and waved the teatowel at him.

'What do you want to know?'

'Um… Let's start with the job. Why are you at Edlers instead of some London bank?'

'Oh, that's easy.' She shrugged and turned back to the dishes, as though reluctant to leave the safety of having something to do with her hands. 'Lying in hospital gives you a lot of time to think about your priorities. It was always my dream to retire back to the bakery at some point.' She paused. 'Put the two together and here I am. In London. As a baker. Ta-da!'

Jared shrugged. 'That's one way of looking at it. Why are you the only baker?'

'Money—I can't afford a professional team. But Trixi begins catering college in September, and is working the rest of the time as my apprentice. What? Don't shake your head like that!'

'Trixi? You must have a lot of faith in her to invest time and money like that.'

'That girl has been taking care of her mother since she was thirteen. She used to come in with her friends on the way to school sometimes, and one day she lagged behind and asked me if she could work a couple of hours in exchange for some bread and muffins. Her mum can't use the oven, but Trixi's a great little cook. We are going to have a blast.'

'I take my hat off to Trixi. I've…known teenage carers. That's a hard start in life. Good luck to her. To both of you, I suppose. It doesn't make life less lonely for you, though.'

Amy started work on the bench and sink, polishing for all she was worth as Jared leant against the worktop in silence, waiting for her to fill the gaps.

'Did you go back to work? After hospital?'

'The company gave me six months' paid medical leave. I came back to England as soon as I had permission to fly. To life in the suburbs with my adoptive mother. I had been shot, and my body needed time to repair itself. The medics had warned me about pushing myself too hard too quickly, and for once I paid attention. I knew I had only just started to come to terms with what had happened to me and what it meant. The hospitals here were great. Only…'

'Go on?'

She dropped the teatowel and stretched out both of her arms before looking at him.

'The company doctor and the cardiologist agreed that my body was not ready for the kind of job I had been doing. Then, out of the blue, Walter Edler and his wife announced that they

were selling Edlers and retiring back to Austria, and they
wanted Maria to go with them to open a guest house. A month
later I moved in. That was almost two years ago, and as you
can see I'm still here.'

'What about your career?'

'My boss, my friends—even my mother thought I would
be back to work and my old lifestyle within six months. They
were wrong. I love it here in London. Some of the happiest
times of my teenage life were spent in that kitchen. I confess
it was a shock, coming back to find the business in such a
mess. The Edlers didn't have the money to invest in it. So I
sold everything I had to make it happen, and I bought the
business. I *am* Edlers Bakery now, and I love it.'

'So you gave it all up? Career? Lifestyle? Everything you
had?'

'I traded up.'

'Any regrets?'

'Some. Little things. I miss having a huge bathroom with
a real bath in it. Expense accounts. And a holiday now and
then would be nice.'

'And where was your boyfriend while all this was going
on? Lucy told me about Ethan—Mike's best man. Was he
with you when you were shot?'

There was an anger in Jared's voice that she had never
heard before. An anger that could mean a spot of trouble for
her ex-boyfriend at the wedding. She had to defuse that
anger—and quick.

'Ethan and I broke up about eight months before I moved
to Chicago. He flew back from Australia as soon as he heard,
and he sat by my bedside for weeks, just thrilled that I was
alive. Ethan is a wonderful friend, but that's all he is.'

Jared stood up and closed the distance between them, and
slid his hands up her shoulders until he was holding her face.

'You are a beautiful woman, Amy Edler. Ethan was a fool
to let you go.'

Amy lifted his hands away and clasped them together on his chest before releasing him.

'He didn't let me go. We both knew that our relationship had come to an end, and we parted best friends—still are, I hope. So don't judge him. That wouldn't be fair. Especially since he's going to be at the wedding on Saturday with his lovely new fiancée. I'm sure she's terrific.'

'Then he's an even bigger idiot. Although it does make me wonder.'

'Um? Wonder what?'

Amy moved back, stretching the fabric of her dress tighter across her chest under her cardigan.

Jared tried not to speculate on exactly how bad the scar truly was, and focused instead on the green eyes looking back at him before replying.

'Oh, I was wondering whether you'd be willing to give another man a chance to show you how stunning you are?'

He was serious. So she inhaled and gave him a serious answer before she had a chance to change her mind.

'Yes. I hope so. I could use a little gratuitous flattery combined with chocs and flowers now and then. Maybe one day.'

'Excellent. Then why not start right now? Today? With me?'

'You don't know how to give up, do you?' Amy said, warning in her voice. 'I said no earlier, and I meant it.'

'Am I not good enough for you? Or are you too afraid you might get used to the idea of being my girlfriend? Maybe even like it?'

'Come on, Jared. You are back in the States next week, and I've seen your diary for the rest of the year. And I have my own business. Thank you for the compliment, but you know it would never work out. And, no, I am not interested in short term relationships.'

'Good. Keep it that way. Because neither am I.'

She looked into those eyes. Fatal mistake. It meant she was

powerless to resist when he moved forward and pressed his long, slim fingers either side of her head, tilting his head to lean in.

His full mouth was moist and warm on her upper lip, and she could not help but close her eyes and luxuriate in the delicious sensation of his long, slow kiss.

Her arms moved around his neck and he moved closer, and she kissed him back, pressing hotter, deeper, the pace of her breathing matching his.

Somewhere at the back of her brain a sensible voice was shouting out that this was not a clever thing to do.

Bad Amy. Very bad.

His lips slid away down her jaw, to kiss her throat so she could gasp a breath.

'Take a chance on me, Amy,' he whispered as his cheek worked its way down the side of her neck to her collarbone. 'I want to be with you, love you, and show you how beautiful you are. Will you give me a chance to do that? Can you learn to trust me that much?'

She forced her eyes open wide enough to see that his own eyes were closed, and his face—oh, his face… She was so going to regret this. One of her arms moved round so that she could move her fingers through his cropped hair. 'I don't know. It would mean that you have to be around for a long time. Can you do that?'

He moved away enough to look at her, his fingers pressing on her back.

'I don't know. But I want to try. Will you give me a chance? Give *us* a chance?'

She looked at him long enough for her stomach to knot up. His eyes were scanning her face as though they were begging her to accept him, give him a chance. There was something in those eyes that went through her skin and penetrated her heart, blowing away any chance of resistance.

There was a lot to be said for giving in to impulses.

Amy found herself grinning back at him, suddenly drunk with the smell, the feel of his touch on her skin, the power of his physical presence.

Her fingertip traced the curved fullness of this man's lower lip, and his mouth opened a little wider at her touch.

Amy stared up at Jared into sea-blue eyes, and knew that he wanted to kiss her again. She focused on his mouth as his long fingers stroked the sides of her face. She had not been so close to a man since Ethan, since before the shooting. It terrified her. And thrilled her.

She wanted him to kiss her. To make the connection she longed for. There was no way she could freeze this man from her life—it had gone too far now for that to happen. Her lips parted and she felt his mouth against hers. Her eyes closed and she let herself be carried away in a breathless dream of a deep, deep kiss.

Tears welled up in Amy's eyes and she tried to turn away as a single bead escaped—too late. Jared wiped it away with his thumb, its gentle pressure stroking her cheek with such tenderness it took her breath away.

How could she have doubted that this man was capable of being gentle and loving?

Yes, loving.

Her gaze scanned the cheekbones of his face, the bumpy nose, coming to rest on the bow of his upper lip above the full mouth that had kissed her for the first time only a few days ago—yet she felt as though she had known him all her life.

Her fingertip moved over the crease lines at the corners of his mouth and eyes, which she knew now were down to more than just laughter. Life had not been easy for this man. His love for his mother and sister had driven him to take risks. If he had become ambitious it was not for his own ego. He had made sacrifices for the people he loved and would do so again.

His hand slid from her cheek into the soft layers of her

short hair, smoothing it back from her face as his lips pressed against her brow, closer. And closer.

Her heart was racing, blood surging in her ears, and she forgot how crazy this was as she closed her eyes and sensed the raw moistness of his lips on one eyelid then the other. One of his hands moved around the curve of her waist, drawing her body closer to his.

The delicious sensation of being wanted as a woman dulled any sense of control she might have had left.

There was only this moment in time. There was only Jared.

She needed him as much as he needed her. How had that happened? And why did it feel so absolutely right to be in his arms, feeling his fingers stroke her back and hair, his lips at the crook of her neck, his chin pressed against her jaw? She knew she would be powerless to resist if the heat of that mouth moved closer.

She wanted him to kiss her again and again, and her head shifted so that she could caress his chin and cheek. Her lips parted and she felt the touch of his tongue on her neck.

Heaven was about to happen.

The pressure of his lips increased as he moved slowly and nuzzled her lower lip, back and forth, until she was lost in the heat of his embrace.

His hand slid from her back inside her cardigan, moving in slow circles on the skin at her waist, sending delicious waves of heat and desire surging through her body.

Her eyes closed with pleasure. He was so good.

There was a movement at her waist. He had started to release her buttons from the bottom up.

She wanted him to. She needed him to. She wanted him to…stop!

Something inside her screamed, and she jerked her face away from his, her eyes catching a flash of his passion, his desire for her, in that split fraction of a second before he realised that she was moving back.

'I thought I was ready for this. Truly I did.' She forced a noisy breath. 'And I'm not. I am so sorry.'

His brows came together, until understanding crept back into the rational part of Jared's brain and he exhaled, very slowly. A couple of times. Before refastening her buttons single-handed.

His arm was still around her waist, and he used his free hand to stroke her cheek as he drew her closer.

She cuddled into his chest, listening to the beat of his heart, knowing that she was the cause of the palpitations and smiling at his need. The smell of his sweat combined with his aftershave filled the air she was breathing.

A bristly chin moved across her forehead.

'I can't guarantee I'll be able to keep my hands off you. You are quite irresistible, Miss Edler. You know that, don't you?'

She grinned, unsure of her own ability to keep her hands off *him* at that moment. But that was not good enough, and Jared lifted her chin so that he could look into her smiling eyes.

'I'll be here when you're ready. I promise.'

She managed to give a gentle nod, before his head lowered and he gave her the sweetest, most loving, lingering, whispering kiss she had ever had in her life.

'Quite irresistible. But it's getting late for a couple of early birds like us.'

His hands dropped to her waist and he stepped back, giving her time to get her breath back.

'I'll be spending time with Lucy and the gang all over the place of England tomorrow, so I probably won't see you again until I pick you up for dinner.'

He leant forward as she nodded her reply, and kissed her on the nose before grinning.

'Try not to kiss anyone else in the meantime.'

CHAPTER TEN

THE sugar flowers were proving to be a real challenge.

Amy bit her bottom lip as she concentrated on curling the ivory sugar paste into a perfect, smooth cone shape, identical to the real lily blossom on the table, then stood back and checked the work.

She smiled.

Not bad. Not bad at all. Lucy was right—Elspeth and the florist *had* created a wonderful bouquet, and the sprays of lilies and yellow rose blossoms would look amazing set against the chocolate icing on the wedding cake. Ivory and pale gold petals, combined with amber and crimson stamens, against rich green leaves.

This cake might *just* be a lot better than okay.

And she desperately needed something to be perfect—especially today of all days.

Then she glanced at the wall clock and gasped. Where had the time gone? She had to finish the roses for the white chocolate centrepiece, and then she needed a few dozen individual rosebuds for the gift bags.

Gulping back her panic, Amy turned back to start on the pale gold roses, and had just started moulding when a familiar male voice echoed from the shop, setting her hand shaking and the butterflies in her stomach turning to swans.

She wasn't supposed to see him until later!

The heat in her kitchen was nothing compared to the heat of the blood pulsing through her veins, hot and fast, in tune with the sudden thumping in her chest—and she was supposed to be trying to keep cool!

Just the sound of his voice made her feel…whole. As though there had been a space in her heart which had been waiting for him to fill it.

He was the reason she'd found herself grinning stupidly to herself without warning for most of the morning, buoyed up by the thought that they would be together again in a few hours. That single thought had been enough to make her sail though her work as though in a dream—the same dream that had kept her tossing and turning all night. Nothing to do with the heat. Nothing at all.

And here he was, simply strolling through the curtain, with the laughter he had shared with Trixi still on his lips.

'Good morning, pretty girl!'

She forced a breath out of her cramped lungs, as her brain unscrambled itself at the sight of him. 'And a good morning to you, handsome man! This is a nice surprise. I thought you were on Lucy duty today?'

Jared pulled out a stool and casually leant his elbows on the metal work table. Amy stared up at him from behind the marble slab she was working on.

'As if I could keep away! I have been sent on a mission. The women in my family know this kitchen is out of bounds, so I am here as a spy. My orders are clear. I have to check on the progress of the famous wedding cake and report back within an hour, or they will go out shopping again! Please save my bank balance! I'm begging you!'

Amy laughed out loud.

'How brave! I suppose that means you have to have physical proof?'

He bared his teeth before nodding.

'Okay, seeing as it's you! Lucy asked for three layers. All

chocolate, but all different! Apart from that, she doesn't want to know until the day.'

Jared exhaled loudly. 'Nice and simple, then! Sorry about that.'

Amy smiled and flipped open the lid of a large container. 'This is the base layer. Smell.'

Jared peered into the round plastic box and inhaled.

'Wow. That's amazing.'

'I started with a dense bitter chocolate buttery cake, then added ground almonds and the finest melted chocolate icing with chocolate liqueur. You serve this one in *very* small slices! The final icing needs to be made tomorrow.'

He peered towards the refrigerator. 'What are the other two layers?'

'White chocolate vanilla sponge on the top. Mocha cappuccino ripple in the middle. Do you think she'll like it?'

Jared chuckled. 'She will be in heaven.' He gestured with his head towards the marble block on the table. 'Are those for the cake?'

'Yellow sugar roses, perfumed with rosewater and vanilla. I'm hoping they will do the trick.'

Jared sat silently watching Amy curling shaped sugar rose petals with tiny tools.

One yellow petal broke into fragments.

'Oh, no. Dried out. Time to call it a day.'

She popped a tiny fragment into her mouth, the tip of her tongue wiping away the crumbs from her lips.

Jared sighed in appreciation. 'Umm. Do that again.'

'Behave!'

But she smiled and lifted the final sugar flower into a wide shallow tray, to join the cream and yellow rosebuds in various stages of bloom.

'That's it.'

She leant across the table and smiled.

'The cakes are ready. Everything is prepped for the icing.

Give me half an hour in the morning tomorrow, and hey presto! We have a wedding cake.'

'I'm no expert, but you've done an amazing job, Miss Edler.'

Amy held out the corners of her white coat and gave him a short curtsey before turning to wash her hands. 'Why, thank you, kind sir.'

Jared nodded in reply. 'I asked the photographer to make sure he spent time on the cake. Think of it as free publicity. You may get a few more orders out of this! Now, I do have one question which is quite crucial to the success of this evening. Indeed, the whole wedding tomorrow could depend on it.'

There was that certain smile and a crinkling around the eyes as he bit his lip. She shrugged off her apron.

'Go on?'

'Are you wearing the gorgeous knickers to the dinner tonight?'

Amy could only laugh out loud. She quickly checked that nobody could see what she was doing, then lifted up the corner of the navy T-shirt to reveal the burgundy silk camisole beneath.

'Do you mean something like this?'

There was a long slow exhalation from the man across the table, who then gave her the kind of look usually reserved for film actors advertising perfumes and fast cars, before taking her hand in his and bringing her knuckles to his lips.

'You look amazing whatever you are wearing. I'll be back around half-seven.'

'Perfect—and thank you.' She gave him a short peck of a kiss on the nose. 'It's going to be a memorable evening.'

It was almost six before Amy was satisfied that Trixi and her friends had everything they needed to run the bakery on their own for the first Saturday in two years when she would not be there in person to supervise.

Of course that was not the only reason she was jittery. For

the next few hours she would be dealing with Lucy Shaw and the father she barely remembered, Lucy's mother and step-father, Mike and his sister Bella, and then, of course, there would be Jared. The brother of the bride. Ethan and his new fiancée would be tomorrow's challenge.

How was she going to make polite chit chat with Jared when they had become…what? Wedding planners? Friends? Lovers? Or as close to it as you could be when you had spent most of the last week together.

Amy stretched out on her bed, closed her eyes, and relived once more the sensuous pleasure of his kisses. No matter that those thoughts had made for very little sleep the night before. In a few hours she would be seeing him again. Being in the same room, touching him. Delicious.

How was it that Jared's aftershave still lingered? His presence was almost tangible in the small space.

Her hand moved to the spot where he had touched her so tenderly, but she snatched it away.

Why now? Of all the times she could have chosen to have a crush, why did it have to be now—and why, oh, why did it have to be on Lucy Shaw's big brother?

A big city executive with a shiny lifestyle and looks to die for?

Sunlight streamed though her open bedroom window onto the contents of her wardrobe. Summer had arrived. And she had nothing to wear on a hot evening to a dinner where at least three of the other guests would be earning six figure salaries.

She had given away or sold most of her good clothing as soon as she'd moved back to London. No point having strap-less dresses when you had to cover up your bosom, and she had no urgent need for designer ballgowns, nor space to store them in this small flat.

Except there was one dress she hasn't been able to bring herself to part with.

Amy reached into her wardrobe and unzipped a garment bag.

Inside was the Chanel cocktail dress Maria Edler had given her as a twenty-first birthday present. The figure-hugging dark green silk and satin gown was gorgeous, with the most stunning beadwork and embroidery Amy had ever seen in her life.

If ever a dress was designed to make a girl feel like a million pounds, this was it. The problem was the neckline—or lack of it. The dress was pleated over the chest and then gathered over one shoulder, leaving the other exposed.

It had been Lucy who'd suggested wearing a lace bolero jacket to cover two inches of exposed scar line, and they had spent two fabulous weekends looking for the perfect piece. The choice had been inspired. And she loved it. A double choker of real pearls, which had belonged to her birth mother, drew attention away from any hint of skin through the lace, onto her slender neck.

Amy pulled on the dress and quickly zipped up the side. It was a perfect fit. Cool. Comfortable. Elegant. The girl reflected in the mirror was the old Amy—ready to take on the world. She peered more closely and leant forward in a cover girl pose. Even contorted double there was only the slightest tip of scar tissue, and even that merged into the ivory of the lace and her pale skin. Yet another reason why she could never be a beach babe again. She had learnt the hard way that scar tissue did not tan the same way as the rest of her skin. And fake tan looked horrible.

But she had to admit that in this dress; there was not the slightest sign of the damage from any view.

Subtle make-up. Her favourite fragrance. Perfect.

She started to unzip the dress and then paused. Why not wear it? Be her old self again? For the next few hours she was going to play the old pretend game and become a sophisticated woman about town.

She was going on a date with Jared Shaw, even if it was for just one night.

And that truly did make her smile.

Her dream was broken by a sharp knock on her door, and a familiar smiling girl popped her head around the edge.

'Hello, baker girl!'

'Lucy! I didn't expect to see you! What a lovely surprise. Come on in. No last-minute jitters, I hope?'

That really made her friend laugh. 'Relax. If I was planning to run off to Vegas I would have done that ages ago. No, I was feeling guilty about not spending more time with you. And. I came to see how you were doing on the recent anniversary of the accident?'

'Thank you but I refuse to feel sorry for myself—especially since there are important decisions to be made. Now come in and sit down, then help me decide about the Chanel. Jared has already seen the blue taffeta, and I hate to be predictable.'

There was a snort from the elegant woman perched on her bed as Amy gave a twirl. 'You do know that he deafened me most of the drive from France with tales about how wonderful you are? I get the distinct impression that my brother wouldn't mind if you turned up in your chef's clothes.'

'I know. He's a special person.' Her voice faltered a little as she gazed out of the window with a dreamy smile, and she flicked her eyes up to Lucy's face as her friend gasped and jumped off the bed to embrace her.

'Oh, Amy Edler. You've fallen for him, haven't you? That's fantastic! Have you told him? I am so pleased for you both!'

'Hold on a minute. I might like Jared—a lot—but his life is in the States,' she said, stunned that she was able to keep her voice calm even now, as she wriggled away. 'It would never work.'

'How can you say that? You were so happy with Ethan! And don't even try to deny it. I was there, remember?'

'You're right. I was happy. We were together for four years, and I'm lucky to have had that time with him. But things are so different now. You know what I mean. You've seen the scar.'

'Then give Jared a chance to show that he is different. He cares about you, Amy, and that is a rare thing for my brother—believe me. He hasn't stopped talking about you. And he's *laughing*. It is rather scary, but I blame you entirely.'

'That's even more reason why I should walk away now, before I see the pity in his eyes when he sees what I look like. I don't know whether I could survive it.'

Amy straightened up as Lucy wrapped her arms around her in a hug.

'It's not right; you deserve the same chance of happiness as anyone else. You've been through so much—you deserve to find love. And maybe, just maybe, my big brother is the one for you.'

'You mean the big brother who is going to miss you like mad once you're a married woman? You *do* know he will never stop wanting the best for you, don't you?'

Lucy shrugged. 'Of course. Goes with the job. It's taken me years to find a man who even comes close to Jared's standards for a suitable husband. Mike has passed the interview, but I suspect there will be routine assessments. I was hoping my brother would find some distraction in a lady of his own. Come on, Amy, give him a chance. Especially now.' There was enough hesitation and regret in her voice for Amy to catch on.

'Now? Why now?'

'There's something you need to know. And I think you had better sit down.'

'I don't like the sound of that. Out with it.'

There was something in Lucy's eyes that demanded Amy's full attention.

'Okay. First, I know that this bakery means a lot to you.

And you've done a fantastic job. Really—I am totally impressed at your achievement.'

A sudden fear shivered through Amy. Whatever Lucy was going to say next was not good.

'You already know that Noodles and Strudels have a five year plan to open cafés all over the UK. What you don't know is that Bill Brooks wants to start building his reputation with six boutique cafés all over London. Starting with…' Her voice faltered, then it all came out in a sudden rush. 'Jared told me that you'd popped into the restaurant we've been working on in Haywood Street, Amy. You know—the place where we used to live as kids. This afternoon Bill Brooks asked if we had a vacant retail outlet in this area. He's thinking of opening a few upmarket Viennese coffee shops. With a bakery on the side. The Haywood Street site could be exactly the sort of thing he is looking for, and he won't rest until he gets what he wants. He's even started making threats if we refuse to sell…'

It took a second for the full ramifications of what Lucy was saying to sink in, and then they hit Amy hard and sent her reeling. The air was punched out of her lungs.

'I'm sorry, Amy. I know this might impact your business. But it doesn't have to be a bad thing! This could be your chance to expand your restaurant supply business instead of relying on passing trade. What do you say?'

Amy pushed herself up from the bed and started pacing the room, her right hand pressed hard against the left side of her chest, feeling the ridge of scar tissue, her head thumping with the powerful thud from her heart.

She had made this bakery her life, and she was tied to it now like a mother to her child. Her young professional customers would love a luxury coffee shop. Only *she* wanted to be the person serving them. Not Bill Brooks. This was *her* dream. He couldn't take that from her. Not now. Not after two years of hard work.

It had never even crossed her mind that another bakery might open nearby.

There were already two supermarkets within walking distance—there was barely enough business to keep her going. Of course that didn't matter when you were an international company with millions of dollars to invest, and able to take a loss.

She needed to think quickly. And think hard.

'How long do I have before he opens? Jared said something about three weeks.'

'That's when I start showing clients around, but Bill hasn't even seen the site yet. Fingers crossed, he may not even like it. What are you thinking?'

'I understand the difficult position you're in, but this?' She waved her hands around in the air. 'This is not only my work! It's my home. This is where I want my children to grow up. I can't let Edlers fail. I just can't. Take this away and I am left with nothing.'

'Who said anything about your business failing? You are a brilliant entrepreneur. Always have been. You can find a way to work around this! Now, please stop pacing and calm down.'

Lucy waited until Amy had moved to the window before going on. 'This is an important new client for us, Amy. Haywood and Shaw need the work if we want to expand. There are hundreds of people who need those jobs, not to mention the suppliers and fitters. And I know Jared feels the same way. He's sacrificed a lot to make our company a financial success.'

'So it'll be a business decision, and that's all there is to it. Is that what you are saying?'

Lucy sighed out loud and came to stand next to Amy, who had her arms crossed, staring out at the traffic in the street below. She could see the houses of Haywood Street over the rooftops opposite.

'Why do you think I came to you tell about it in person?'

She clasped hold of Amy's upper arms and physically turned her round, gulping down emotion when she saw the tears on her friend's face.

'Please don't cry. You'll get *me* going. I wanted you to find out from me before I tell the others at the party tonight.'

'That doesn't change the fact that I might have another bakery opening up on my doorstep in the next few months. A lot of my customers live on Haywood Street, and they have to walk past your new site before they reach me. I don't know how to compete against a coffee shop and patisserie selling the same food that I make. Don't you see? This changes everything. And what about my little girl?'

She looked at Lucy's white face, closed her eyes and exhaled, slowly, before opening her eyes and hugging her friend—who should be excited and happy about her wedding, not worried about a friend's bakery.

'I'm sorry Lucy. Ignore me. I'm so tired. Thank you for telling me in person. Only, please send my excuses for your party tonight. I can't pretend to be enjoying myself in idle chatter. Not tonight.'

Her friend frowned in distress. 'Oh, no—you don't turn me down now. You *have* to come to this dinner.'

Amy took her hands. 'Don't worry. I'll be fine with some sleep, and we'll have a fabulous day tomorrow. Whatever happens in our work, you know I only want you and Mike to be happy. Nothing will change that.'

'Jared will kill me.'

'He doesn't know you're here?'

Lucy shook her head. 'Jared is still out ferrying our things from the hotel to his apartment. He doesn't know about the call from Bill Brooks. That was going to be my big surprise announcement tonight. The good news before the bad.'

Amy looked up with her mouth open.

'Oh, you have *bad* news? Well, I can hardly wait!'

Lucy took a breath and spoke in a nervous rush, her words

running together in her panic. 'I invited my dad to give me away and he's accepted. My father will be walking me down the aisle tomorrow instead of Jared.'

She looked up at Amy with terror on her face. 'Now do you understand why I need you there? It's not for me, it's for Jared. I have really hurt him this time.'

The answering machine was beeping away as Jared strolled into his apartment, and he casually pressed the 'play' button as normal. His luggage was at the hotel and Lucy was now fully installed in his guest room, so there was at least an hour to relax and catch up with his latest projects before getting changed to pick up Amy.

At that moment he caught sight of himself in the hall mirror. A grinning face looked back at him, and he knew exactly who was responsible.

It had been years since he had wanted to spend time with anyone so badly. There was the dinner tonight, then the whole day tomorrow at the wedding. Good food and wine. Perhaps a little dancing at the reception? The girl deserved some time off for herself.

One thing was pretty certain. He was falling for a London baker. He hadn't seen that one coming!

Then the voice that came out of the answering machine echoed around the empty hall and wiped that grin away in an instant, stopped him dead. Frozen to the spot.

'Hello, Lucy darling. Dad here. I can be at the restaurant around eight tonight, if that's okay. Give me a call if there's a problem. Looking forward to seeing you all again. Bye for now.'

Jared collapsed onto his sofa and pressed his right thumb and forefinger tight against the bridge of his nose, before slapping both hands down hard onto the cushions.

He had heard Eric Shaw's voice exactly twice in the last eighteen years.

The first time he had been fourteen years old, and his

father was being bundled into the back of a police car by two burly officers. Just as the door had closed, the man he had idolised for his whole life had leant forward and said the few words that had burnt into his brain. 'Look after your mother and sister for me. I'm relying on you, son.' His face had been so pale. Scared. Intense. Resigned.

The door had closed, and he'd been sped away. Jared had run down the street, focusing on the back of his father's head through his tears, until he'd heard his mother's voice calling him back to a house which didn't belong to them any more.

He had tried so hard to understand why his father had not wanted him to attend the law court. No bail. No prison visits. He'd had a problem understanding why his letters were never answered, and he simply hadn't been able to believe that his photographs and cards were returned unopened. No telephone calls. No Christmas presents. No sign that his adored father cared about them, about how they were surviving in the horror that was their new life, without the house and expensive school they had become used to.

It was as though their father had been lifted out of their lives and had stopped caring.

Of course his mother had tried to shield himself and Lucy from the horror of empty bank accounts and credit card bills. But she hadn't been able to shield Jared from the newspapers.

With a young boy's curiosity about what his father had done to be charged with embezzlement, it had not taken him long to discover the truth. A lifetime of hard drinking and visits to casinos with colleagues after work had become a problem. Eric Shaw owed money. The kind of money he would never be able to pay back. He had already remortgaged their house and cashed insurance policies and investments without telling his wife. There was nothing else to sell. So he had betrayed and robbed the clients who'd trusted him with their life savings and investments.

Jared exhaled. Slowly. And glanced around his apartment. He had bought this place with cash from his personal account.

No loans. No debt.

The New York apartment was in Lucy's name, together with all of the other apartments in her building, which she leased to executive tenants. Her little pension fund, as she liked to call it. Except they both knew that it was far from little. Their mother had remarried a wine merchant who owned a small estate in France and the château that came with it. She certainly did not need Jared to take care of her now.

From the very beginning Haywood and Shaw had used the profit from one sale to invest in the next project. Expansion was paid for by hard work with clients who needed someone reliable to develop major projects.

Clients like Bill Brooks at Noodles and Strudels.

Was this apartment Jared's home? Or just a serviced flat he used as yet another hotel room? Lucy had already decided to move her personal possessions back to New York when she returned from honeymoon. Where would that leave him?

An unfamiliar twinge of something close to regret crept into Jared's mind at that thought. Lucy had been only half joking about starting a family before she got too old to enjoy her kids.

What had he got to offer any woman except a weekend here and there away from his non-stop life? A woman like Amy Edler, for example? The bakery was her life, her work and her home. She couldn't simply drop everything to fly out to Miami or Aspen for a few days at short notice simply because he had a gap in his schedule.

Amy deserved better than that. A lot better.

He wiped one hand over his face, then scratched his head with the fingers of both hands, front to back. Perhaps Amy was right. Maybe Lucy had the right to invite who she wanted to her wedding. One way or another he was going to have to meet his father and be civil to him, for her sake.

There was only one problem.

The second time he had spoken to his father had been almost three years ago, when the man had had the nerve to walk into the offices of Haywood and Shaw and ask his son for work and 'a bit of cash' to see him clear.

He hadn't got the work, but he had got the cash.

Lucy didn't know that he had been paying his father to stay away from them. To leave them alone. Well, all that was all about to change. Because if Eric Shaw told the truth for once in his life, Jared didn't know if his sister would ever forgive him.

He might have made the biggest mistake of his life.

What he had done would hurt her very badly.

'Okay if I use the bathroom before I go out, Amy?' Trixi popped her head around the bedroom door. 'You look nice. What a lovely dress!'

'Thank you. And please—help yourself. Can you lock up when you leave? I need to take a walk and clear my head before the party.'

'Sure. Are you okay? You look worried. Not like you.'

Amy smiled as she slipped the bolero around her shoulders. 'Tired. I will be so pleased when this wedding is over and things are back to normal next week. What are you and your mum up to this evening?'

Trixi beamed out a smile. 'Mum is having some of her friends round for a drink and a DVD, and they're staying over, so I have the night off.' She pulled on a strand of lank light brown hair and stared at it for a second. 'Can I stay here overnight? I thought I might change my hair again. This is so *boring*!'

'Of course you can. I'll see the results when I get back tonight. Have a good time!'

There was enough of a breeze to waft warm air through Amy's still-damp hair as she strolled along the pavement on a busy Friday evening rush hour.

She had to get out of the flat and away from the organised chaos of the bakery workload. Away from the telephone, e-mail and personal visitors like Lucy, who could hit you with bombshells. There was only one quiet spot where she *knew* that she could find peace on her own at seven p.m. on a Friday evening—where the world would not be able to find her.

Amy paused long enough to check where she was, crossed the street between stationary cars, and started walking, faster now, down Haywood Street towards the Haywood and Shaw sign.

With a bit of luck the side gate at a certain building site would still be unlatched...

Chanel dress or no Chanel dress, she would climb over the fence if she had to. Then and only then would she try and decide whether she truly wanted to eat dinner with the Shaw family and enjoy herself.

Twenty-fourth of June. Seven p.m. The second anniversary.

She knew Lucy and Mike had not forgotten, but Lucy had far more urgent things to focus on—such as her wedding, and whether her father and brother would end up in the hospital and a police cell tonight after trashing the restaurant.

Of course Mike had been captain of the judo team at university. Black belt. If Jared or Eric Shaw dared to upset his beloved Lucy he might feel inclined to give a personal demonstration of his skills.

Well, maybe the three men could share the same police cell and talk it out before morning? Then smile sweetly in the church tomorrow.

Oh, Lucy.

Amy shook her head and smiled as she strolled up to the side entrance of the building. The clean-up team had done a fantastic job and the car parking area was now spotless. No builders' vans, no hammer drills or saws. The workers had already left.

Just as she'd expected the gate was unlocked, and without a glance backwards she lifted the latch and slowly strolled through into the sunlit garden where she had spent precious minutes with Jared only a few days before. Her own piece of heaven. While it lasted.

'What exactly did Amy say?'

Lucy shrugged and peered into her capacious handbag. 'Please thank Jared for me, but I will make my own way to the restaurant tonight.' She looked up him. 'Is that a problem, sweetie? You do know you will get wrinkles if you frown like that!'

'The poor girl is probably working late to finish that famous cake of yours! I hope you feel guilty!'

Lucy shook her head. 'No, that's not it. Something about needing to find a quiet spot to clear her head. She wasn't too happy when I mentioned that Bill Brooks was interested in the Haywood Street site. I suspect I might get a call some time in the next hour with some excellent excuse why she can't come to dinner with us. Not that I blame her.'

Jared whipped around. 'You didn't *tell* her that he was interested!'

'I explained it was only a provisional visit. Nothing has been signed. She knows that this is our business, Jared. Besides, I went round to tell her in person in case it was mentioned this evening. She deserved to hear it from me first!'

'Well, you got that right. Great timing, Lucy! You couldn't have waited until after the wedding? Monday, perhaps?'

'Stop groaning. I went round to wish her a happy birthday and it came out. I wasn't planning to make a formal… What?'

'Today is Amy's birthday? Is there anything else you are not telling me?' He groaned and glanced at his watch. 'You might have mentioned this yesterday, sis. We'll need to stop at a shop on the way and buy cards and flowers. Drat.'

'Of course. You don't know.' Lucy lowered her bag and

swallowed down her emotion. 'This isn't her actual birthday—that's in September. Amy was shot exactly two years ago today. Jared? Where are you going? It's almost half-seven! Jared?'

There was a distant, 'Call you!' from him as he was halfway out of the door, before it closed behind him.

It was turning out to be quite a day! thought Lucy. With a bit of luck he would be too busy worrying about Amy to ruin the dinner party when their father walked in—with his father of the bride speech in his hand.

CHAPTER ELEVEN

AMY sat back against the warm stones in the semi-dusk of the late evening sun and slowly closed her eyes.

In this secluded corner under the conservatory canopy she was hidden away, invisible, in a private world where no one could see her from the street or the other houses.

She desperately needed to calm down and think, but her mind was too busy trying to process the thousand and one things that had broken through her normally quiet existence in the past week.

Why hadn't Jared told her that Bill Brooks might be interested in this place? He knew she was struggling. There had to be some good reason.

A sudden noise from the gate brought her out of her dream. Surely the builders had gone home for the night?

She leant forward to see who it was at the same moment as a familiar pair of black shiny shoes stepped forward onto the patio tiles.

Jared Shaw.

Simply the sight of this man hit her so hard that she leant back against the wall, not caring that her lace bolero jacket would be ruined. It staggered her that one look at his handsome face could send her senses into a stomach-clenching, mind-reeling, heart-thumping overdrive.

What was it about him that made her feel like a schoolgirl on a first date?

Her heart raced to see him, as if she had dreamt this marvellous creature up out of her imagination.

Jared smiled and strolled the few steps towards her, looking sexier than any man had a right to be in a stunning dark suit and dove-grey shirt selected to highlight the blue in his eyes. Expensive. Groomed. A man who lived and worked in the world she had left behind. The world he would be going back to in a few days.

And there was not one thing she could do about that.

Yet seeing him now—tall, muscular, so relaxed—she simply wanted to hold him close and relive those precious moment in his arms, feel his kiss on her lips once more before the inevitable happened and he returned to his real life thousands of miles away.

Amy stretched forward and smiled back. Waiting for him to speak. As he came closer she saw something more than relaxed confidence in that smile. Confusion. Regret.

Oh, yes. She recognised *that* look only too well.

Lucy must have told him that this was the second anniversary. Great. *Just great.*

Her hand started to move towards her chest, and the scar tissue, but she instantly blocked the move and turned it into a casual brush through her hair away from her forehead.

'Hello,' she said. 'I hope I'm not trespassing, but you did tell me to come back any time I liked. Looking for me?'

Here it comes, she thought. *He doesn't know how to handle it.*

'I'm not used to being stood up. Came as quite a shock.'

She turned away for a fraction of a second to pick up her evening bag. 'Lucy came round to my flat to let me know about Bill Brooks.' Her voice stayed calm, despite the thumping storm of confusion and anger building in her chest. 'Was that why you introduced us the other evening, Jared?

To give me a taste of what I should expect? You could have warned me.'

'No. Lucy didn't have the complete story today. I've already offered Bill a much better site on a high street the other side of town.'

Her mind reeled with the impact of what he had said, and she slid back down onto the hard stone step and looked up at him in astonishment.

'Just like that? Bill Brooks isn't interested in this café any more? How did that happen?'

'Simple. I told him that I had already earmarked this site for a new client who is happy to serve slow food. One I met this week in London.' Jared tapped his forefinger against his lower lip. 'He got me thinking, though. Maybe this unit *does* need a luxury café. It would draw customers to the other shops and provide a focal point for this street. Ideally, I would love to create a real Viennese coffee shop with a fresh artisan bakery on the side. The kind of place where regulars could relax on a Sunday morning over a newspaper and a pastry. That sort of thing. Any idea where I might find someone interested in running that sort of business? It could be a winner!'

Someone in a nearby house opened a window, and the sound of piano music echoed out across the patio garden. But Amy did not hear the Chopin. She was way too busy fighting to keep breathing in a controlled manner.

Jared lowered his body onto the stone next to her and stretched out his long legs, his splayed fingers only inches from hers.

One side of his throat was lit rosy pink by the sun as he twisted his body around to face her, apparently oblivious to the damage he was causing to the fine fabric of his trousers, which stretched to accommodate the muscled thighs below.

'What do you say, Amy?' he said, his pale blue eyes locked onto her face, his voice low and intense, anxious.

'Would you be interested in moving here? Say yes. Say that you will trust me.'

Trust him? Trust him with her life, her future. Her love?

'There is a great apartment on the second floor, with a huge bedroom, and I could talk with the builder to make sure you had the biggest bath we can find!'

'Why me?' she asked, her voice almost a whisper.

His response was to slide his long, strong fingers between hers and lock them there. Tight. The smiling crinkly blue eyes locked onto hers and a wide grin of delight and happiness cracked his face.

'I'm going to be spending a lot more time in London over the next twelve months, and there is nobody else I would rather spend time with than the woman I'm looking at right now.'

The café.

Her dream.

Her love.

This amazing man was offering her the chance she had been waiting for, working for every second since she'd walked into Edlers Bakery all those years ago. This man whom she had only met a week ago, yet felt she had known all of her life.

He was holding her dream out to her. All she had to do was say yes and it would be hers.

Her back made contact with the wall. Her sides pressed against the stone.

Amy inhaled a deep breath, trying to process the words. His body was only inches away from her own, leaning towards her, begging her to hold him, kiss him, caress him.

She swallowed hard and tried to form a sensible answer. 'London? I don't understand. I thought you couldn't wait to leave this place?'

'It dawned on me that I have an excellent project team in New York who are desperate to show me what they can do without my constant interference. There is plenty of work for me here. And of course there is one final reason why you are the only person I want to run this café.'

Amy let out a long, slow breath as his fingertips moved over her forehead and curled around the layers of her short hair before caressing her scalp. There seemed to be something fascinating on the side of her head.

'What is that?'

'It's not every day that I have a chance to make a girl's dream come true. I want to make this happen for you. Will you let me into your life to do that?'

Suddenly it was all too much, too soon to take in.

Take care of her? Make this happen for her?

She looked up at the lovely building surrounding her and was instantly transported into a happy dream of what life would be like. Edlers. The café. And maybe the tantalising prospect of playing with her adopted children in this lovely garden.

Oh, no. The reality of what he was proposing hit her hard.

Idiot girl! Who was she kidding? She had to work long and hard just to pay the lease on Edlers. How could she possibly afford this amazing new site? It was so far out of her league it was a joke, and the sooner she laid that dream to rest the better.

By reaching up and taking both of Jared's hands in hers, she managed to regain some control of herself before words were possible.

'This is a wonderful site, Jared, and I would love it here. But you know I don't have the money to run two shops, and I don't want your charity. Or your pity.'

His fingers meshed into hers, and he raised one hand to his lips and gently kissed her smooth knuckles before replying.

'Then let me invest in your business. I know a good opportunity when I see one, and from what I've seen we would make a great team. You can do this, Amy. I know you can.'

The pressure in her chest was almost too much to bear as she looked into his face and saw that he meant it. He believed in her!

'You would do that? You would come back to this street and this building? Even after everything you've told me?'

'If it meant I could be with you? In a heartbeat.'

His presence was so powerful, so dominating, that she slid her fingers away from below his and pushed herself away, out of the corner and onto the patio stones, on unsteady legs.

Only she moved too fast, and the sleeve of her lace bolero jacket snagged on the corner of a piece of stonework and pulled taut. The sleeve was dragged away, pulling the lace from her chest. Exposing one side of her scar.

She gasped in horror and turned away from him, pulling on the lace to cover herself. But it was caught fast, and as she jerked hard the handmade lace started to tear and pull.

The ridge of scar tissue was burning hot, alive, raised under her fingers, and she gasped in short, fast breaths.

'Amy? Are you in pain? What can I do?'

Jared was standing next to her now, his voice filled with concern, and she felt the touch of his hand on her waist.

'Wait. Let me do that for you.'

'No. I don't want you to see me.'

But he was already there in front of her, slowly stroking the jacket even further down her exposed shoulder so that there was no strain on the precious cloth and the jacket lifted easily away from the stone.

Amy immediately tried to pull the jacket back into place, but his fingers meshed with hers and held them to his own chest as it rose and fell under her palm.

She forced herself to look up, into his face, and what she saw there took her breath away. Any doubt that this man cared about her was flashed away in an instant.

No pity, no excuses, no apologies. Just a smouldering inner fire. Focused totally on her.

And without thought or hesitation she lifted their intertwined fingers and pressed Jared's palm flat against her chest, against the raised scar tissue which lay beneath the green silk, so that his fingertips were resting on her bare skin. The heat of his touch, its gentle pressure, warmed her body like nothing ever had before.

Soft fingertips pressed against the scar tissue. She could sense the pressure. Trembling, hesitant, but loving.

He was the flame that had set her world on fire. Nothing would ever be the same again.

Jared looked into perfect wide green eyes, the colour of a sky-reflecting sea, and was lost.

All the clever words of persuasion he had practised in the taxi cab drifted away like thin wisps of cloud in the breeze, taking his inhibitions and fears with them.

He had found someone he wanted to be with, in the last place on the planet he had ever wanted to come back to. Over the years, he had convinced himself that a few thousand miles and a successful business were enough to steer him away from the path that led here. To the house he had watched being demolished. To the same patch of land where he had spent the most miserable eighteen months of his life.

How could he have known that the path to happiness led right back to where he had started? How ironic was that?

Bill Brooks and the business were not important any longer.

All that mattered was this woman looking at him with tears in her eyes. This was where he wanted to be. Needed to be. With Amy.

He dared not speak and break the magic of that moment, that precious link that bonded him to Amy for this tiny second in time. But he could move closer, closer to that stunning face. Those eyes filled with the love and tenderness he had only imagined was destined for other men. And now she was here. And he loved her.

Finally. It had happened. He had known lust and attraction. But this sensation was so new, so startling, that the great Jared Shaw floundered.

He was in love.

The lyrics of every song he had ever heard suddenly made perfect sense.

Without thinking, he moved his hands slowly up from her chest to her throat, to cradle her soft and fragile face gently, his fingers spreading out wide. As her eyes closed at his touch he had to blink away his own tears as he moved closer, so that his body was touching hers, his nose pressed against her cheek, his mouth nuzzling her upper lip as his fingers moved back to clasp the back of her head, drawing her closer to him.

She smelt of every French perfume shop he had ever been into, blended with spice and vanilla, and something else in her hair. Coconut. The overall effect was more than intoxicating. He wanted to capture it for ever, bottle it, so that he could relive this moment in time whenever he wanted.

And then her mouth was pressing hotter and hotter into his, and his pulse was racing to match hers. Both hands were on his chest, then around his neck, caressing his skin at the base of his skull so gently he thought he would go mad with wanting her, needing her to know how much he cared.

Maybe that was why he broke away first, leaning back just far enough so that he could stroke the glint of tears away from her cheeks.

'Why didn't you tell me this was the second anniversary?'

She smiled weakly against the turmoil inside her heart. 'Each day is a new day for me. A new start. I should have died on that street. Instead of which I am here with you.' She pressed her head into his shoulder as his arms wrapped around her body, revelling in the touch of his hands on her skin, the softness of his shirt on her cheek, the way his hand moved to caress her hair.

'Some of us carry our scars on the inside, Amy. I don't want the world to feel sorry for *me*. Pity *me*. Can you understand that? I want us to have a happy ever after. Let me work with you to make this place the magical café you always wanted. I want to be part of your life.'

He was kissing her now, pressing his soft lips over and over again against her throat, tilting his head so he could reach the sensitive skin on her chest.

The fingers that had been splayed on her scar slid slowly against her hot, moist skin and gently lifted away the shoulder strap of her dress so that his mouth could cover the spot.

Her eyes closed and she leant back just a little further, arching her back, supported by the long fingers which had slid down her back to her hips. Amy stopped breathing and inwardly screamed in frustration that the dead nerves in the scar were letting her down. His hot breath warmed the skin either side, and she knew that he was watching her. Looking at her. And he was not repelled. Her heart and mind sang.

His voice was hoarse, low, intense, and warm with laughter and affection, and something much more fundamental.

'I have an idea.'

'Umm?' was all she could manage. His mouth was still moving on her throat.

'Let's hold our own celebration. Just the two of us. Your place is closer. I'm sure my sister will understand.'

Amy closed her eyes tight shut and focused on the sound of her own breathing, as the doctors had told her to. Only it was rather difficult when the man she wanted to be with was holding her so lovingly, keeping her steady on her wobbly legs. Her toes clenched with tension inside her shoes.

He was tempting her. Tempting her so badly she could taste it. She wanted him just as much as he wanted her.

Lucy! The dinner!

Amy chuckled into his shoulder. 'Are you mad? She would never forgive us!' Then she dropped her head back, so he would have to stop kissing her. 'Maybe…' she took a breath '…you could escort me home afterwards, Mr Shaw?'

The air escaped from his lungs in a slow, shuddering hot

breath against her forehead, and he lowered both hands to her waist.

'It would be my pleasure. Do you think they would notice if we skipped dessert?'

'That sounds wonderful. Although I will have to insist on having an early night. My alarm is set for four a.m.'

The brilliant grin grew wider, although she could still sense the thumping of his heart in tune with hers. 'I'm sure we could manage that.'

Then the reality of what he was asking hit her hard. 'Oh, I'm sorry, Jared. I completely forgot. Trixi is staying at my place. She might be almost 18, but I promised her mother that I'd keep an eye on her. But we'll have the wedding tomorrow, and the rest of the weekend.'

As soon as the words had left her mouth she regretted them. The man who had been holding her so lovingly, unwilling to let her move out of his touch, stepped back. Moved away. Not only physically, but emotionally.

The precious moment was gone. Trampled to fragments.

'We need to talk about your plans to adopt… I…'

His face contorted with discomfort, pain, and closed down before her eyes. The warmth was gone, and she cursed herself for being so clumsy. She had lost him.

It took her a few seconds to form the words of the question she had to ask. She was almost too afraid of what the answer would be.

'You don't want children, do you?' Her voice quivered just enough to form the syllables, but she held her breath until he answered.

Jared shook his head slowly, and his chin dropped so their foreheads were touching. His breath was hot against her skin as the words came stumbling out. 'No, my darling, I don't want children. Not my own, and certainly not someone else's. I never have. I want you and only you. Can you understand that?'

Amy took a slow breath and squeezed her eyes tight shut,

blinking away the tears. 'And I want you. So very much. I had given up hope of ever finding someone to love. Only I so want to have children of my own. You would be a wonderful father, Jared. I just know it.'

'A family? Oh, Amy.'

His back straightened and he drew back, physically holding her away from him. Her hands slid down his arms, desperate to hold onto the intensity of their connection, and her words babbled out in confusion and fear.

'Let's not talk about it now. You have such a lot to celebrate over the next few days, when your family is all together for once.'

He turned away from her now, and sat back against the sun-warmed wall, one hand still firmly clasped around hers.

'My family? Do you mean Lucy and Mike? My mother and her new husband? Or my father? The prodigal.'

Amy took a breath before answering. 'Your sister forgave him. I admire her for that.'

Jared ran his fingers back from his forehead to his neck. 'So do I. They say love is unconditional. She loved him once. I know that.'

'And you?'

'He was the man I wanted to be. I idolised him. And he let me down. I could never do that to a child of mine. And, no, I can't forgive him for what he did.'

There was such pain in his voice, such bitterness, that the contrast with the loving man she had just been talking to was hard to comprehend.

'Jared! That's such a hard thing to say!'

'It's the truth. That's what my father means to my family. Hardly the best example for any son.'

'Then talk to him about it, face to face, and get it over with. I can help you if you want me to.'

He looked at her now. 'Thank you for the offer, but that is not going to happen.'

The world stilled and the temperature of the air seemed to cool, as though a cold wind had blown between them.

She stepped back and folded her arms across her chest, closing down, moving away from the hot flames that would burn her up if she kissed him again, held him close to her again.

'Oh, Jared. I am so sorry. But Lucy needs both of you in her life.'

'They don't need him. I'm all they need.'

She raised both her hands in the air so that Jared could not grab hold of them.

Amy shook her head. 'It took me ten years to forgive my parents for being killed in that stupid car crash and leaving me alone in this world. Both of your parents are still alive, and they love you. To me, that's something you should celebrate.'

When she had gulped away the burning sensation in her throat she looked into those wonderful eyes, so full of concern, and told him the truth—because nothing else would do.

'You're breaking my heart, Jared. Is it wrong to want a family? To give a child a loving home in this hard and cruel world? Can't you see that is part of my dream?'

She paused, and then spoke very slowly, with something in her voice he had never heard before and did not ever want to hear again.

'Now, don't worry. I'll get through the wedding tomorrow with a smile on my face. I can do that much for Lucy. Only it might be best to stop this now. You have your life thousands of miles away, but this is my home, and I don't want to give it up. If you care about me, then let me go, Jared. Let me go.'

The only thing that stopped Jared from running after her was the heartbreak in her words and the unavoidable truth that he *did* care about her enough to stand, frozen, and watch her walk away.

CHAPTER TWELVE

AN IRRITATING buzz broke through the angry haze as Amy stomped down the pavement in her favourite pale green silk shoes. Going nowhere in particular in a hurry.

Her cellphone! It was probably Lucy, making sure that she had the correct address for the driver. Jared would not dare call!

Her shoulders immediately hunched in stress, and there was a telltale increase in her pulse rate again. Not good. She could *do* this. She was holding it together. She was calm. She could take a simple phone call from a friend.

Flicking open the handset, Amy squinted at the caller ID, then looked at it again. That was Trixi's number! Strange…

'Is that you, Trixi? How's it going?'

All thoughts of Jared were wiped from her senses the moment she heard the sound of sobbing at the other end of the line. The girl was hysterical, gasping in breaths of air, incomprehensible.

'It's okay, Trixi. I'm here. Tell me what's happened. Are you hurt? Where are you?'

'My mum. She's fallen, and there is an ambulance coming to take her away. She's all I have. Please—please come to the flat. Please, Amy. I need you. *Please*.'

It was almost eleven that night before Amy staggered to the back door of her bakery and turned the key.

Trixi was okay. Her mother had some nasty bruises on her arms and face, and was badly shaken, but nothing was broken or sprained, and the paramedics had eventually agreed that there was no need for her to go to the accident and emergency department.

It had been an emotionally exhausting end to an exhausting day, and all she wanted to do was go to bed and forget today had ever happened. Tomorrow was going to have to take care of itself.

As soon as Amy got to the front door she heard a sickening sound. She made the mistake of swinging the back door open and switching on the kitchen lights.

It was the sound of water pouring from the ceiling onto the hard tile floor, already dark with water and littered with the remains of the kitchen ceiling.

She screamed, and a piece of plaster peeled off the wall and splashed on the floor.

Thank goodness for the large battery torch she kept by the back gate. She gingerly turned the electric lights off and checked the torch.

Obviously the water was coming from her flat, so she ran up the stairs. And screamed again. She couldn't help it. It was even worse upstairs. The bathroom was at least two inches deep in water and floating vinyl tiles. There was a stream running from the bathroom across the hall and disappearing into the gaps between the warped and curled hardwood flooring of her hall. The original polished bedroom floor looked like wood tone corrugated roofing.

She waded into the bathroom, grateful that she had chosen not to wear sandals, and trying to ignore what was happening to her lovely shoes as her toes started to become moist.

Both shower taps were gushing water into her tiny shower tray.

The tray was overflowing because a hand towel was blocking the overflow. Discarded containers of make-up and clothing littered the floor. And the carton from a box of hair dye.

Trixi had been in the middle of changing the colour of her hair.

She closed her eyes and swallowed down anger and frustration. Trixi must have been rinsing the dye from her hair when she'd taken the call from her mother, run out in panic, and left the water running. The discarded towel had floated against the tiny overflow drain.

Oh, Trixi.

The sensible part of her started telling her calmly that she should turn the water supply off. Then the mains electricity. Especially since the water had now soaked her shoes and she was standing in a puddle.

The crazy woman part of her started shouting that she needed to call a plumber—*now*!

The only man who would know what to do, and the men to do it, was somewhere in this city feeling sorry for himself—because she had dumped him after he had offered to make her dream come true.

And he was the best kisser.

He had taken care of his mother and she had left him. He had taken care of his sister and now she was planning to leave him, and desert him on her wedding day for his father.

And now she had told him that she did not want to see him again.

A four-inch square of bathroom tile fell off the wall right in front of her, and sloshed into the water around her shoes.

Amy dug into her bag and found her cellphone by torchlight. She dialled the number, closed her eyes.

Please be there.

Please answer.

Please don't throw the phone out of the window when you see who is calling you. Please take this call.

The only voice in the world she wanted to hear whispered, 'Amy?'

'I need your help. Please.'

Jared swung the car into the rear yard of the bakery, having broken the speed limit several times in the last ten frustrating minutes, and left the engine running so that its headlights shone directly into the kitchen.

He jogged across the space, oblivious to the devastation as water and plaster dripped down from the ceiling above his head.

'Amy? Are you there?' And then he saw the light of her torch moving from a corner.

'Over here! Watch the floor—it's a slippery mess. I've had to turn the power off.'

She was wearing rubber boots, a fluorescent yellow workman's jacket with her green chiffon dress sticking out below it, and a baseball cap promoting a brand of butter. And at that moment she was the most beautiful woman he had ever seen in his life.

He swept her up, holding her body tight, tight, before tilting his open mouth onto hers in a hot, hot kiss.

'Are you okay? Tell me. Are you hurt?'

'I'm fine. A little damp, but fine. Can't say the same for my bedroom floor, which is.' She never got the chance to continue since Jared grabbed her around the waist, pulling her into his arms, and held her pressed against his jacket so that she could feel the urgent beat of his heart as he kissed the top of her head.

'You terrified the living daylights out of me. Please don't ever do that again. I love you, Amy. I love you so much.'

He cupped her face with both of his hands, his thumbs wiping away tears and water from her cheeks, then poured into his kiss the passion and devotion, the fear and doubts that came with giving your heart to another human being.

'I've waited all my life to say those words to the woman I love. I didn't expect to be saying it standing in a flooded kitchen, with plaster falling on my head, but it doesn't change a thing. I am so in love with you.'

'Oh, Jared. I wasn't sure you would come. I was such an idiot. Can you forgive me? Especially about your dad.'

'Better than that. The world-famous Haywood and Shaw clean up squad are on their way, with my new apprentice plumber. He's a bit older than the other lads, but I'll give him a chance.'

'Seriously?' she asked, stunned.

He nodded. 'Seriously.' His thumb still moving across her cheek. 'Our children are going to need a grandfather from *my* side of the family.'

'Oh, Jared. Do you mean it? Yes? Oh, I love you so much.'

He closed his eyes and pressed his forehead to hers, his entire world contained within his arms.

They were still standing there, kissing passionately, when more car headlights lit up the yard and car doors opened and closed in rapid succession, the sound of loud male and female voices breaking into their private world.

Amy looked into the laughing eyes of the man she loved, and smiled back as he turned towards the lights. 'The cavalry have arrived. You do know that we shall never be free of them, don't you?'

'They're the ones who pointed out how much our kids will be loved. I don't need the cavalry. I only need you.' And with that she stood on tiptoe to wrap her arms around his neck and lock herself into his kiss.

'Hey, Amy. Put my brother down. You have no idea where he has been. I hope you're not coming to my wedding dressed like that!'

'Nice outfit. The wellies almost match the Chanel in this light. Mind if I take your photo? It will look great in the wedding album!'

'Good one, Bella! I'll take some copies.'

'Amy...Where's my cake?'

More headlights and shouts broke the evening air, and the full impact of the devastation that had been her home and kitchen hit Amy head-on. She leant even closer to Jared as they watched three men she had never seen before jog into the kitchen with emergency lighting.

'Tell me the truth. Is it a wreck? Do I still have a business?'

'Nothing that we can't fix. Together. If you'd like that?'

'I'd love it.'

'Me too. I'll make your landlord an offer he can't refuse. In the meantime, I happen to know a vacant bistro in Haywood Street which is looking for a tenant.'

'But what about your work? New York?'

'Lucy and Mike have agreed to take over that part of the business. Plus Nell Waters offered me a new job this week. Could be challenging.'

'Difficult?'

'Very. Based in London, actually.' He grinned. 'Within walking distance of this kitchen and the woman I've fallen in love with. And all the strudel I can eat. How could I say no?'

EPILOGUE

AMY snatched a calming breath of warm, perfumed air as Elspeth checked for the third time in fifteen minutes that Amy's coronet of tiny yellow rosebuds was not in danger of going *anywhere* soon, before moving back to Bella, whose hair had been gelled, sprayed and pinned into submission.

The long skirt of Amy's oyster silk sheath dress shimmered in the warm sunlight, and she was grateful for the embroidered chiffon jacket that covered the new bruises on her arms from carrying crate after crate of cooking equipment and cake boxes from the ruin of her kitchen as Jared and his team had worked through the night to rescue her possessions.

It had taken four journeys from the bakery to Jared's penthouse to save what she had needed, but it had been worth it. The three cakes she had delivered to the hotel only an hour ago in the SUV were—in Bella's opinion as well as her own—awesome.

Lucy had peeked into the boxes in her hair rollers, and made a sound somewhere between a gasp and a satisfied smiling sigh of relief and pleasure. The French dessert chef at the famous name hotel had simply crossed his arms and shrugged at her, before telling her she was okay. Which to Amy was a result, since she had been wearing Jared's rolled up tracksuit bottoms, a chocolate stained T-shirt and white hotel slippers at the time.

The sound of a powerful engine brought them to the window of the church vestry, and Elspeth switched into even higher gear as Frank slid the beautiful Rolls dressed in white ribbons to a gliding halt.

One minute ahead of schedule.

Jared would be delighted.

Amy sighed out loud as Frank helped Lucy step out of the car. She looked so stunningly beautiful and happy that every second of their work over the last week seemed worth it a thousand times over.

Jared.

The last few hours had passed in such a blur of hairdressers, make-up girls and dressmakers that Amy had begun to wonder if she'd dreamt the previous evening, when he had held her in his arms as they declared their love.

Poor Jared had barely had time to admire the lingerie drying in his bathroom before his own penthouse had been declared out of bounds and he had been bundled off to the hotel in the middle of the night, with Mike and the rest of the family, to dry out for a few hours.

And yet here they were. Elspeth gave a final twitch to the stunning train on Lucy's dress, and glanced swiftly over their matching bouquets of lilies and yellow roses, before nodding that they were ready.

This was it.

Lucy glanced back to Amy over her shoulder and beamed the gloriously happy smile of a happy bride before taking the arm of her handsome, debonair father. Above them the church bells pealed out over London, and at some hidden signal the church door swung open. The opening bars of the 'Wedding March' drifted out of the high-arched stone entrance.

With a rustle of the heavy silk taffeta gown on the stone paving, Lucy and her father stepped out into the narrow aisle and began their stately way down the church filled with friends and family, who turned *en masse* with smiling faces to share their happiness.

Bright June sunlight beamed through the stained glass window above the altar, so that the air was tinted with subtle pinks, lilacs and blues tones, contrasting with the garlands of cream lilies, bright ivy and yellow roses decorating the ends of the pews. The sweet heady perfume of the flowers lifted with their every step.

Amy walked slowly behind Lucy and her father, her eyes instantly searching out and fixing on the tall man standing to the right of Mike and Ethan.

Jared was wearing tailored morning dress, and looked so handsome as he grinned at her that it took her breath away to know that his smile was not just for his sister—but for her. In his eyes she was beautiful.

Every step down the aisle was taking her closer to this re-markable man that she loved.

Of all the people in this world he had chosen her as the one woman he wanted to spend his life with.

This man loved her.

He was her new family.

He was where her heart was.

In those strong arms she knew she'd found a home and love for the rest of her life.

Perhaps this wedding had not turned out too badly after all.

* * * * *

*Celebrate 60 years of pure reading pleasure
with Harlequin!*

To commemorate the event, Harlequin Intrigue® is
thrilled to invite you to the wedding of The Colby
Agency's J. T. Baxley and his bride, Eve Mattson.

That is, of course, if J.T. can find the woman who left
him at the altar. Considering he's a private investigator
for one of the top agencies in the country—the best of
the best—that shouldn't be a problem. The real setback
is that his bride isn't who she appears to be…and her
mysterious past has put them both in danger.

*Enjoy an exclusive glimpse of Debra Webb's
latest addition to*
**THE COLBY AGENCY:
ELITE RECONNAISSANCE DIVISION**

THE BRIDE'S SECRETS

*Available August 2009
from Harlequin Intrigue®.*

The dark figures on the dock were still firing. The bullets cutting through the surface of the water without the warning boom of shots told Eve they were using silencers.

That was to her benefit. Silencers decreased the accuracy of every shot and lessened the range.

She grabbed for the rocks. Scrambled through the darkness. Bumped her knee on a boulder. Cursed.

Burrowing into the waist-deep grass, she kept low and crawled forward. Faster. Pushed harder. Needed as much distance as possible.

Shots pinged on the rocks.

J.T. scrambled alongside her.

He was breathing hard.

They had to stay close to the ground until they reached the next row of warehouses. Even though she was relatively certain they were out of range at this point, she wasn't taking any risks. And she wasn't slowing down.

J.T. had to keep up.

The splat of a bullet hitting the ground next to Eve had her rolling left. Maybe they weren't completely out of range.

She bumped J.T. He grunted.

His injured arm. Dammit. She could apologize later.

Half a dozen more yards.

Almost in the clear.

As she reached the cover of the alley between the first two warehouses she tensed.

Silence.

No pings or splats.

She glanced back at the dock. Deserted.

Time to run.

Her car was parked another block down.

Pushing to her feet, she sprinted forward. The wet bag dragged at her shoulder. She ignored it.

By the time she reached the lot where her car was parked, she had dug the keys from her pocket and hit the fob. Six seconds later she was behind the wheel. She hit the ignition as J.T. collapsed into the passenger seat. Tires squealed as she spun out of the slot.

"What the hell did you do to me?"

From the corner of her eye she watched him shake his head in an attempt to clear it.

He would be pissed when she told him about the tranquilizer.

She'd needed him cooperative until she formulated a plan. A drug-induced state of unconsciousness had been the fastest and most efficient method to ensure his continued solidarity.

"I can't really talk right now." Eve weaved into the right lane as the street widened to four lanes. What she needed was traffic. It was Saturday night—shouldn't be that difficult to find as soon as they were out of the old warehouse district.

A glance in the rearview mirror warned that their unwanted company had caught up.

Sensing her tension, J.T. turned to peer over his left shoulder. "I hope you have a plan B."

She shot him a look. "There's always plan G." Then she pulled the Glock out of her waistband.

Cutting the steering wheel left, she slid between two vehicles. Another veer to the right and she'd put several cars between hers and the enemy.

She was betting they wouldn't pull out the firepower in the open like this, but a girl could never be too sure when it came to an unknown enemy.

Deep blending was the way to go.

Two traffic lights ahead the marquis of a movie theater provided exactly the opportunity she was looking for.

The digital numbers on the dash indicated it was just past midnight. Perfect timing. The late movie would be purging its audience into the crowd of teenagers who liked hanging out in the parking lot.

She took a hard right onto the property that sported a twelve-screen theater, numerous fast-food hot spots and a chain superstore. Speeding across the lot, she selected a lane of parking slots. Pulling in as close to the theater entrance as possible, she shut off the engine and reached for her door.

"Let's go."

Thankfully he didn't argue.

Rounding the hood of her car, she shoved the Glock into her bag, then wrapped her arm around J.T.'s and merged into the crowd.

With her free hand she finger-combed her long hair. It was soaked, as were her clothes. The kids she bumped into noticed, gave her death-ray glares.

They just didn't know.

As she and J.T. moved in closer to the building, she grabbed a baseball cap from an innocent bystander. The crowd made it easy. The kid who owned the cap had made it even easier by stuffing the cap bill-first into his waistband at the small of his back.

Pushing through the loitering crowd, she made her way to the side of the building next to the main entrance. She pushed J.T. against the wall and dropped her bag to the ground. Peeled off her tee and let it fall.

His gaze instantly zeroed in on her breasts, where the cami

she wore had glued to her skin like an extra layer. A zing of desire shot through her veins.

Not the time.

With a flick of her wrist she twisted her hair up and clamped the cap atop the blonde mass.

"They're coming," J.T. muttered as he gazed at some point beyond her.

"Yeah, I know." She planted her palms against the wall on either side of him and leaned in. "Keep your eyes open. Let me know when they're inside."

Then she planted her lips on his.

* * * * *

Will J.T. and Eve be caught in the moment?
Or will Eve get the chance to reveal all of her secrets?
Find out in
THE BRIDE'S SECRETS
by Debra Webb
Available August 2009
from Harlequin Intrigue®

We'll be spotlighting a different series every month
throughout 2009 to celebrate our 60th anniversary.

LOOK FOR
HARLEQUIN INTRIGUE®
IN AUGUST!

To commemorate the event, Harlequin Intrigue® is thrilled
to invite you to the wedding of the Colby Agency's
J. T. Baxley and his bride, Eve Mattson.

Look for *Colby Agency: Elite Reconnaissance*

THE BRIDE'S SECRETS
BY DEBRA WEBB

Available August 2009

www.eHarlequin.com

HIBPA09

Harlequin® Historical
Historical Romantic Adventure!

From *USA TODAY* bestselling author
Margaret Moore

THE VISCOUNT'S KISS

When Lord Bromwell meets a young woman on the mail coach to Bath, he has no idea she is Lady Eleanor Springford—until *after* they have shared a soul-searing kiss!

The nature-mad viscount isn't known for his spontaneous outbursts of romance—and the situation isn't helped by the fact that the woman he is falling for is fleeing a forced marriage....

The Viscount and the Runaway...

*Available August 2009
wherever you buy books.*

BRENDA JACKSON

ONE NIGHT WITH THE WEALTHY RANCHER

Maverick County Millionaires

Unable to deny the lingering sparks with
the woman he once rescued, former detective
Darius Foster is determined to keep his
distance…until her life is once again in danger.
Forced to be together, they can't deny their
desire for one another, but they soon realize
that there is more between them than lust.

Available August wherever books are sold.

Always Powerful, Passionate and Provocative.

SD76958

Silhouette®

nocturne™

USA TODAY bestselling author

LINDSAY McKENNA
THE SEEKER

Delia Sebastian and U.S. Army captain Jake Tyler are
assigned to travel back in time to locate the missing pieces
of an ancient relic. They land in ancient Rome, where the
search turns deadly and their attraction for each other is
stronger than ever. Will they be able to escape the past to
realize their love in the present?

Look for book #1, available August 2009 wherever books are sold.

THE SLAYER BY CINDY DEES—*September*
THE AVENGER BY PC CAST—*October*
THE PROTECTOR BY MERLINE LOVELACE—*November*

TIME RAIDERS

Bestselling authors Lindsay McKenna, Cindy Dees,
P.C. Cast and Merline Lovelace come together
to bring to life incredible tales of passion
in a brand-new four-book miniseries.

www.silhouettenocturne.com
www.paranormalromanceblog.wordpress.com

**Stay up-to-date
on all your romance
reading news!**

The Inside Romance
newsletter is a **FREE**
quarterly newsletter
highlighting
our upcoming
series releases
and promotions!

Go to
eHarlequin.com/InsideRomance
or e-mail us at
InsideRomance@Harlequin.com
to sign up to receive
your **FREE** newsletter today!

You can also subscribe by writing to us at: HARLEQUIN BOOKS
Attention: Customer Service Department
P.O. Box 9057, Buffalo, NY 14269-9057

Please allow 4-6 weeks for delivery of the first issue by mail.

IRNBPA0109

REQUEST YOUR FREE BOOKS!
2 FREE NOVELS PLUS 2
FREE GIFTS!

HARLEQUIN® *Romance*®

From the Heart, For the Heart

YES! Please send me 2 FREE Harlequin® Romance novels and my 2 FREE gifts (gifts are worth about $10). After receiving them, if I don't wish to receive any more books, I can return the shipping statement marked "cancel." If I don't cancel, I will receive 4 brand-new novels every month and be billed just $3.84 per book in the U.S. or $4.24 per book in Canada. That's a savings of at least 15% off the cover price! It's quite a bargain! Shipping and handling is just 50¢ per book.* I understand that accepting the 2 free books and gifts places me under no obligation to buy anything. I can always return a shipment and cancel at any time. Even if I never buy another book, the two free books and gifts are mine to keep forever.

114 HDN EYU3 314 HDN EYKG

Name	(PLEASE PRINT)

Address	Apt. #

City	State/Prov.	Zip/Postal Code

Signature (if under 18, a parent or guardian must sign)

Mail to the Harlequin Reader Service:
IN U.S.A.: P.O. Box 1867, Buffalo, NY 14240-1867
IN CANADA: P.O. Box 609, Fort Erie, Ontario L2A 5X3

Not valid to current subscribers of Harlequin Romance books.

**Are you a subscriber of Harlequin Romance books
and want to receive the larger-print edition?
Call 1-800-873-8635 today!**

* Terms and prices subject to change without notice. Prices do not include applicable taxes. Sales tax applicable in N.Y. Canadian residents will be charged applicable provincial taxes and GST. Offer not valid in Quebec. This offer is limited to one order per household. All orders subject to approval. Credit or debit balances in a customer's account(s) may be offset by any other outstanding balance owed by or to the customer. Please allow 4 to 6 weeks for delivery. Offer available while quantities last.

Your Privacy: Harlequin Books is committed to protecting your privacy. Our Privacy Policy is available online at www.eHarlequin.com or upon request from the Reader Service. From time to time we make our lists of customers available to reputable third parties who may have a product or service of interest to you. If you would prefer we not share your name and address, please check here. ☐

HR09R

You're invited to join our Tell Harlequin Reader Panel!

By joining our new reader panel you will:

- Receive Harlequin® books—they are FREE and yours to keep with no obligation to purchase anything!
- Participate in fun online surveys
- Exchange opinions and ideas with women just like you
- Have a say in our new book ideas and help us publish the best in women's fiction

In addition, you will have a chance to win great prizes and receive special gifts! See Web site for details. Some conditions apply. Space is limited.

To join, visit us at

www.TellHarlequin.com.

HARLEQUIN *Romance*®

Coming Next Month

Available August 11, 2009

**Have a holiday romance with Harlequin in August
and get swept away by our gorgeous, sun-kissed heroes!**

#4111 CATTLE BARON: NANNY NEEDED Margaret Way
Scandalously gate-crashing her ex-fiancé's wedding costs Amber her
job! Then brooding rancher Cal MacFarlane makes her nanny to his
baby nephew. Once the media frenzy dies down, can Cal convince
Amber to stay?

#4112 HIRED: CINDERELLA CHEF Myrna Mackenzie
After an accident that shattered her spine, Darcy's made a new life for
herself as a chef. Her most recent position might be temporary, but her
gorgeous boss has other ideas....

#4113 GREEK BOSS, DREAM PROPOSAL Barbara McMahon
Escape Around the World
Aboard his luxury yacht, Nikos isn't looking for love. But sharing the
breathtaking beauty of the idyllic Greek islands with his pretty new
employee is driving him crazy!

#4114 MISS MAPLE AND THE PLAYBOY Cara Colter
Primary-school teacher Beth Maple is cautious and conventional. Yet
when stand-in dad Ben appears at the school gates with his good looks
and confident swagger, Beth is starstruck!

#4115 BOARDROOM BABY SURPRISE Jackie Braun
Baby on Board
When pregnant Morgan arrives at billionaire Bryan's office looking for
her baby's father, two things become apparent: she has mistaken him for
his late brother, and she's in labor—in the boardroom!

#4116 BACHELOR DAD ON HER DOORSTEP Michelle Douglas
Jaz is back in her hometown, determined to face her old flame Connor
with dignity—and distance. But she hadn't reckoned on Connor being
even more irresistibly handsome—or a bachelor dad!

HRCNMBPA0709